Unwanted Danger

Unwanted Danger

*** *Previously published under the title Discarded Heart*

Years ago, Caleb Faulkner left the little town of Applewood for the excitement of Chicago and the chance to build a career with the FBI. Unfortunately it also meant leaving behind Micheala Adams, the woman he loved and adored. All the success in the world couldn't fix the emptiness he felt inside without her.

Michaela gave up her chance at a lifetime with Caleb to stay in Applewood to nurse her dying sister and care for her nephew. She doesn't regret her decision but sometimes in the middle of the night she thinks about what might have been.

His career in ruins, Caleb is back in town to lick his wounds and start again. When he and Michaela run into each other it's agonizingly awkward and more emotional than he expected. The less they see of each other the better.

Unfortunately, their hearts have other plans.

Unwanted Danger

Danger Incorporated

Book Nine

BY

OLIVIA JAYMES

www.OliviaJaymes.com

Chapter One

WITH A TIRED grunt Caleb Faulkner heaved the last cardboard box onto the kitchen counter and wiped the sweat from his brow. It was a hot and humid day and his t-shirt stuck to his skin from his exertion. He should have hired someone to do this but he hadn't been thinking all that clearly when he'd planned this move.

The small Craftsman style house would be home for the next three months or so while his mother recovered from a mild stroke and the federal government obliterated over a decade of hard work.

His good friend Jon Rudnick placed a lamp on the floor before heaving his large frame into a leather-cushioned easy chair. Jon had been a close friend for a long time and had recently retired from the Navy SEALs to open his own security firm with a few friends. "I think that's the last of it. Hell of a way to spend Labor Day."

"Doing hard labor? I can't thank you enough for the help. This would have taken me all damn day if you hadn't been here. Dad's not getting any younger and he shouldn't be hefting boxes if I can help it. I'm trying to get him to retire but he says he'd be bored as hell."

Caleb grabbed two beers from the refrigerator and handed one to Jon who rubbed the chilly bottle on his forehead before twisting off the cap. "It's no trouble. Ali's got a late summer cold and she's taking it easy this weekend. I'll pick her up some chicken soup on my way over to her place."

"Looks like you're all domesticated now." Grimacing, Caleb took a long draw on his beer and sat down on the couch. "But you look happy."

Jon picked at the label on the bottle, wet from condensation. "I am happy, so that makes one of us. You can punch me if you like but you don't look too happy for a man that's moving back to his hometown and his roots."

That was the problem with old friends. They knew a person inside and out.

Dammit.

"Let's just say that a month ago the thought of moving back to Applewood was the furthest thing from my mind. Then one case gets blown out of proportion and I'm on indefinite suspension while I'm being investigated. They think I botched the case and all because some rich guy got busted and he's got all his wealthy cronies throwing their weight around in Washington and making things difficult for me at work. This wasn't how I pictured my life."

Caleb had always assumed he'd be with the FBI until he retired. Until this incident his career trajectory had only gone one way.

Up.

"Your life or your career?"

Shrugging, Caleb took another drink from the already half-empty bottle. "What's the difference? My career is my life."

Jon shook his head, a smile playing around his lips. "There was a time I would have said the same."

"But not now?"

"Not now. I have a life and I have a career. There's more to me than being a former SEAL. I don't want to be one of those guys that hang out in the parking lot of their old high school talking about their glory days. That's a shit way to live."

Caleb sat back and propped his feet on the coffee table. "It's easy for you to say. You have a new career with your security business. I've got nothing. I told Dad that I'd help him with his carpentry jobs but I can't imagine doing that for the next twenty or twenty-five years. Day in and day out. No excitement. No adrenaline. Don't tell me you could live without that. You crave it just like I do."

"Sure, but there are other ways to get that. Take up sky diving or something. You can do whatever you want. The only one holding you back is you. I have to ask—do you even want to go back to the FBI after getting jerked around like this?"

A good question, and one Caleb didn't have the answer to. Yet. But the subject was never far from his mind. When the investigation into the handling of the Morton case was complete and Caleb was found to have handled it by the book, he'd have to make the call of whether to stay here in Applewood or go back and try and salvage what he could of his career. He'd worked too damn hard to simply chuck it away without a second thought.

"It's what I do," Caleb said after a moment. "I'm not sure I can do anything else. My childhood dreams of being a cowboy or an astronaut are long gone."

Jon took the last swallow from the beer bottle and set it on the end table. "You're too tall to be an astronaut but you might find work as a brick wall."

At six-foot-four and two hundred and thirty pounds, Caleb wasn't a small man. Even in high school he'd been a big kid, playing quarterback on the football team because he could easily see over his front line. His size had never been a handicap. Not in the military and not when he'd signed up with the FBI. He'd used it well to intimidate those around him but it wasn't much of an advantage now that he was back in his hometown. What was he good for now?

Helping little old ladies reach the top shelf at the grocery store.

Jon levered up from the chair and walked a few steps away to the large picture window overlooking the quiet street. Caleb had rented this house because of its proximity to the town square, not the serene small town atmosphere the tree-lined street promoted. He was used to concrete, metal, and glass punctuated with the roar of engines and the wail of sirens. Add in some gritty exhaust fumes and he was in heaven.

The closest he would probably come here in Applewood was a neighbor burning their leaves.

"Have you seen her?" Jon asked, his gaze still directed outside so he didn't see Caleb's shoulders immediately stiffen. But Caleb had no doubt his friend had heard him suck in a breath at the mere suggestion.

Caleb didn't even have to actually hear her name. Her memory was enough to knock him sideways.

"No. No, I haven't. But I doubt I can avoid her. This town just isn't that big."

Jon turned and crossed his arms over his chest. "What are you planning to say to her when you do?"

Caleb laughed but it sounded strangled in his throat. "You're assuming I have a plan. I don't. I have no idea what I'm going to say. I do know what I'm going to do. Or at least what I hope I'm going to do. I'm not planning to make a fool of myself. She doesn't need to know how she affects me all these years later. I'll be polite and friendly. Hopefully we can give each other a wide berth."

It had occurred to Caleb more than once that Michaela might not want to see him even more than he didn't want to see her. The last time they'd spoken hadn't been sunshine and puppy dogs. When he'd walked away that final day Michaela's face had been wet with tears as she clung to the cotton fabric of his shirt, her eyes begging him not to go.

But he had. There was no changing the past. No rewriting history.

"That's probably for the best," Jon agreed, tossing his empty in the trash can Caleb had set up last night when he'd received the keys. "Unless of course you're here to stay. That would make everything different."

"It wouldn't change a thing." Caleb shook his head, too many memories making his insides churn. "You know the old saying about making your bed and lying in it. This is one of those times. Just because I stay – and I'm not saying that I am – wouldn't make Michaela any more inclined to forget the past. That ship sailed long ago."

"Maybe she still feels the same."

Not a chance in hell.

"She stopped loving me years ago. Smart girl."

Some things were meant to be and some not. Michaela was meant to live in a small town. Caleb was meant to fight wars in deserts and chase bad guys for the government. Their dreams had made sure they would never have a future together. It was all for the best.

Jon slapped Caleb on the back and smiled. "I know you'll be okay, but just in case I'm inviting you to the poker game me and a few friends put together when we can. Cards, beer, and artery-clogging food. Are you in?"

"Wouldn't miss it. Text me with the details."

"Will do. I better get going. I want to check on Ali."

Caleb stood and followed Jon to the door. "Thanks again for all your help. And the poker invitation."

"What are old friends for?" Jon laughed as they stepped out, the heat and humidity almost taking Caleb's breath away. Autumn couldn't come soon enough. "I'm glad you're back even if you aren't. Let me know if there's anything else you need help with."

There wasn't anything anyone could do. Caleb had to deal with the mess of his life all by himself. He couldn't see far into the future, but if he didn't get straightened around there wouldn't be much of one.

He'd screwed up everything important in his life. At age forty this was officially Round Two of Caleb Faulkner and he didn't intend to lose.

Chapter Two

"SO WHAT ARE you going to do?"

Michaela Adams picked up the menu and pretended to peruse it so she could have a few precious seconds before answering. Her friend Charlotte, however, wasn't fooled in the least. She plucked it from Mika's fingers and slapped it down onto the worn formica table. The two of them were sharing a late lunch at the Applewood Diner. Their kids were playing together while Charlotte's husband Ron babysat them while also simultaneously watching a football game.

Their lunches were a tradition that had started years ago to allow the mothers a few hours out of the house. Of course it had changed a little over time as the children had grown older but the point was still the same – girl talk time.

"That menu hasn't changed in thirty years and you always get the fried chicken on Sundays. Stop stalling. Have you seen him yet?"

Mika let out a long suffering sigh and shook her head. Charlotte was like a dog with a bone and she wasn't going to let this go until Mika spilled her guts all over the booth they were occupying.

"No. I've been busy and I bet he has too. Frankly, he's only rented that house for three months. I might get lucky and never see him while he's here."

Charlotte rolled her eyes and groaned. "In Applewood? You're kidding, right? There's no way you can avoid him and you know it. You'd have to become a hermit and we both know Alex isn't going to let you do that. What are you going to say to Caleb when you see him after all these years?"

Mika had no idea and had spent the better part of the week trying not to think about it. It dredged up way too many memories. Good, bad, and downright painful.

"How about 'nice to see you and welcome back.' That sounds neutral. What Caleb does now doesn't affect me one way or the other, Char. That was a long time ago. I'm older and hopefully a hell of a lot wiser. It takes more than a good looking smile for me to find a man attractive."

The waitress brought their drinks and took their order, leaving them alone once again.

"You loved him once," Charlotte pointed out. "You didn't get the closure you needed and now he's back. I just thought you might want to talk to him and put this behind you once and for all."

Mika sputtered, the ice cold water choking her for a moment. "Closure? I think his leaving after college graduation and joining the Navy could be called closure. Add in the day years later when he told me he was taking a job with the FBI in Chicago and I think he nailed that sucker shut. He said goodbye, Char. He couldn't wait to get out of Applewood. It was his dream and I always knew that. I was fooling myself to think he'd stay here for me."

"You could have gone with him. Alex wasn't your responsibility. Your parents practically begged you to follow Cal."

Mika remembered those heartbreaking conversations well. Her older sister Sarah had been ravaged with cancer at the time, unwilling to take chemo or radiation while pregnant. By the time Alex had been born the tumors were too far gone and Sarah had passed on less than six months later. The only thing Mika could do for her sister was promise to raise Alex as her own. She hoped that she had succeeded these last eight years.

"Love isn't always enough to make things right. He needed to go and I needed to stay."

"He said he'd do the long distance thing."

Mika carefully placed the glass down on the table and tried to keep a hold of her emotions. The memories she'd pushed away for so long were coming back one by one. Deeply painful, they sliced at her heart and abdomen, almost making her double over. All these years later her heart still ached as she remembered the earnest young man she'd loved so deeply. He'd been hell bent to make something of his life. Ambitious, smart, and hardworking, she always knew he'd be successful. She'd just fooled herself to think it would be in Applewood.

He was born to excel. To achieve. An excellent student. Star athlete. He'd blinded her with his movie star good looks and hefty doses of charm. He'd been her own personal prince except that she didn't get a happily ever after with him. She was left behind while he chased rainbows. She'd tried to make it work but in the end the fabric of their relationship slowly shredded until they were hanging by a string.

He'd been climbing the ladder of success while she'd been changing diapers and warming bottles, worlds apart from one another.

"And it was a huge disaster. He wanted the big city and excitement. I needed to stay here and take care of Sarah—then when she died I became Alex's mother. It was a mess and it's my own fault. He never made any secret of what he wanted."

She'd thought she could somehow change his mind if she'd loved him enough. But young women often believed what they wanted to when they were in love.

And she had loved Caleb. So very much. But she had loved her sister and Alex too.

"He's back. Maybe he'll stay."

Fiddling with her fork, Mika shook her head. "He's got a three month lease on that house. He's here because his mother is sick from what I heard. When she feels better he'll leave again."

Alice Faulkner had recently had a mild stroke and was recovering well. But it was nice to see Caleb spending more time with his family. He'd barely been back to Applewood since he left for good almost eight years ago.

"Maybe he's changed."

That statement made Mika laugh. "Charlotte Williams, you're a married woman with three children and you of all people should know how often men change. It's a myth perpetuated by women's magazines and hopeless romantics."

Charlotte sighed and then grinned. "I can't even get Ron to change the empty toilet paper roll so I guess you have a point."

"I plan to stay far away from Caleb Faulkner," Mika declared, that familiar ache in her heart making her want to curl up and cry. "Nothing good can come from spending any time with him."

Charlotte never had a chance to reply as the bell over the diner door chimed announcing a new customer. Caleb and his father Abe stood in the doorway, scanning the crowded restaurant for an empty table.

Cal looked the same although older. His dark hair was clipped short and she could see just a touch of gray at his temples. His skin was tan but his jaw was still just as square and his face just as handsome. He'd put on muscle in the intervening years, his shoulders wide and imposing although he moved gracefully for a man that large. A memory of the two of them dancing at the senior prom flitted unbidden through her mind and she had to squeeze her eyes shut for a moment as what felt like a knife pierced her chest.

Well, crap.

So much for her plan. Looks like she had to face him whether she liked it or not.

Right now she didn't like it one bit. She simply wasn't ready to see him again.

✦ ✦ ✦

CAL'S LUCK HAD held for almost seven straight days.

All week he'd managed to somehow avoid running into Michaela despite the fact that the town was small and everyone knew everyone else. He'd assumed she was avoiding him and could only feel grateful. She was saving them both an awkward encounter.

But now here she was, sitting in a booth near the back of the diner with her friend Charlotte. They'd been friends since grade school and had even double dated with Cal and Michaela on more occasions than he could count. He'd heard she'd married Ron Williams, her high school sweetheart, and lived in that new housing development that had sprung up on the edge of town.

Abe Faulkner nudged Cal's elbow. "There's an empty table near the back, son."

Right next to Mika.

She'd grown more beautiful in the years since he'd last seen her. There was a maturity to her face that hadn't been there before. Her eyes were still that amber color that darkened when she was angry and turned almost pure gold when she was aroused. Her auburn hair still hung in waves down her back and Cal couldn't help the rush of relief that she hadn't cut it short like so many women as they grew older. He could vividly remember running his fingers through those silky strands before tracing her high cheekbones, her skin like satin under his palms.

His heart racing and his stomach twisting, all Cal wanted to do was turn around and get the hell out of there. He wasn't ready for this. He might never be.

How Cal felt at the moment apparently didn't matter because his father had brushed past him and was striding toward the booth, sliding onto the vinyl seat before picking up a menu. Sucking air into his lungs, Cal had no choice but to trail behind, his gaze firmly on the old black and white tile floor and not on the woman who had broken his heart years ago. He couldn't let a chance encounter with her upend the peace he'd fought so hard for. He'd finally moved on with his life.

He already knew she had.

Cal barely glanced at the menu, his appetite gone. His chest ached and he couldn't seem to catch his breath. Even though he'd been home for a week he still wasn't prepared for the punch in the gut he'd felt the moment he laid eyes on her. He'd been shot in the leg and it hadn't hurt this badly.

"You gonna puke?"

Abe's slightly dry tone snagged Cal's attention. The older man was looking at his only son with a mixture of sympathy and impatience. He'd mentioned Michaela once this week and Cal had quickly shut him down.

There was an "I told you so" in Cal's not too distant future.

"No, are you?" Cal quirked an eyebrow at his father who chuckled and studied the menu. Knowing Abe Faulkner wasn't done, Cal waited quietly. There was no point in moving on to another topic when the patriarch of the family wasn't finished with this one.

"Did you think you would see her and it wouldn't mean anything?" Abe finally asked, not unkindly. "Did you think it wouldn't hurt or that you wouldn't think about the past?"

Cal didn't want to talk to his father about...feelings, for fuck's sake. He'd go hunting with him or shoot hoops or even sit and watch a football game, but talk about how he'd gone out and gotten himself drunk as a skunk the day she'd told him she wasn't coming to Chicago after all?

Not going to happen.

"I don't feel anything and it was bound to happen sooner or later. I told you we've both moved on."

Abe nodded absently and set the menu down on the table. "I'm glad to hear that, son, because I've volunteered both of us to help out building the attractions for the town haunted house. It's for a very good cause and I assist every year."

Son of a bitch. The wily fox had easily cornered Cal and from the grin on his face had immensely enjoyed doing it.

Assuming nothing had changed, Michaela volunteered to help create and run the annual haunted house for the local children's charity. Her grandmother and mother had both done it and Michaela joined in when she was quite young. If Cal kicked up a fuss about this it would look damn selfish.

Time to man up and deal with his past.

"Of course I'll help out. Like you said, it's for a good cause."

Cal would make a point to put as much distance between them as possible. The worksite was large and perhaps he could keep his head down and avoid a confrontation.

Abe rubbed his chin, a smile still playing on his lips. "The best that could happen would be for the two of you to talk this out." Cal's father leaned forward, his expression turning grave. "She's been through a lot since you left, with Sarah passing on and then both her parents a few years later. Those are things no one should have to deal with. She's all alone now raising that boy and she sure doesn't need the extra stress of you and her scowling at each other for the next three months. Think about her for once, son. Put her first."

Cal reared back at his father's plain speech. "What do you mean 'think about her for once'? Are you saying I've never put her first? I loved her, Dad. More than you can imagine."

Cal had started this conversation not wanting to talk about his feelings and here he sat…talking about them.

Shit.

"I think you loved her as much as you were capable of. But you didn't love her enough."

"What's enough?" Cal shot back, anger making the back of his neck hot.

"Enough to stay," Abe said calmly. "Enough to put her needs first. Just don't make her life difficult. She's had more heartache than anyone should have."

With a sigh of defeat Cal slumped in the booth. He didn't want to cause Michaela any more pain. He'd hurt her when he left but in the end he'd hurt himself more. Still, she didn't deserve even one moment of discomfort because of his presence. She'd stayed in Applewood for good reasons.

"I'll stay out of her way," Cal stated firmly. "I don't want to interfere in her life either."

"That's not what I meant, son. Not at all. But I can see you aren't ready to listen to what I have to say. Why don't we just figure out what we're going to order and eat? The sooner we can get back to your mother the sooner her sister can leave and drive her own husband crazy."

His mother's sister Beatrice liked to talk. She liked an audience for it as well and had a flair for drama. She could drive Abe crazy within ten minutes of stepping into the house.

"Mom's going to be okay."

Abe opened the menu, effectively shielding himself from Cal's gaze. He acted like he wasn't worried but Cal knew better. His father would be lost without Alice Faulkner. "Well, of course she is. It's good that you're here though. She's always saying you don't come home often."

Often? That was a parental understatement. He usually flew

his parents out to Chicago instead.

"I think I'll have the fried chicken." Cal didn't bother to reply to the subtle dig about his absence from Applewood. He didn't want to argue with his father today. Or tomorrow for that matter. "And some of that apple pie for dessert."

Still keeping his gaze averted from Michaela, Cal and his father gave their order to the waitress. When she left something inside of Cal made him want to reassure Abe that he wasn't here to cause trouble. He was here for his mother. And for a place to figure out what he was going to do with the rest of his life. It was just his luck those two things happened to coincide.

"Listen, Dad, I know you're worried that I'm going to upset Michaela but I don't want to do that. I'm here to visit and help. I want to make things better for you guys."

Abe's eyes narrowed and he shook his head. "You don't get it at all do you, son? I'm not worried about what you're going to do. I'm worried about you. *You.* I can see that my boy isn't doing too well. When you're ready to talk about it your mother and I will be here. Until then I'll keep my peace."

With that he began to talk about the town's preparations for the Autumn Festival but Cal barely heard a word of what he said. He was still dealing with the shock that his father knew his life was fucked up. If he was this transparent while undercover he would have been dead long ago.

But he couldn't deny that it felt good to have someone worry about him. When he was a kid his mother would make brownies when he had problems. Cal doubted that there was a brownie in the world that could solve all the issues that were running around his brain.

He'd have to solve them all on his own.

Chapter Three

"THIS LOOKS PRETTY spooky, Mom. Where is it going to go?"

Mika's eight-year old son Alex was holding up a glow-in-the-dark skeleton. Both the boy and the bony figure were wearing big grins that made her reach out and ruffle Alex's dark hair.

When he smiled he looked so much like Sarah.

"Here." She pointed to the parlor room on the blueprint she had rolled out on the long table. "It will hang from the chandelier and dance."

Alex's eyes lit up as he studied the sketch. "This is going to be so cool. Can I really help this year?"

Her son had a bad case of *I wish I were older.* Last year she'd allowed him to hang around a few times during construction but mostly she'd kept him away, not wanting to deal with nightmares she was sure would follow. But clearly he'd inherited her love of all things macabre. Yesterday she'd found him playing with a hairy black plastic spider, not scared in the least.

"Yes, you can really help but be sure to stay out of the workers' way when they have tools. I don't want you or anyone else for that matter to get hurt."

Alex could help paint sets but she drew the line at chainsaws.

"I will," he promised. "Can we have pizza when we get home?"

Placing her hand on her hip, she leaned down to look her son in the eye. As fast as he was growing she wouldn't need to do that much longer. "How many questions are you going to ask me?"

Alex giggled, not fooled in the least by her mock stern tone. It was a running joke between them that he was constantly asking questions. They'd become much more complicated as he grew older and lately he'd stumped her a few times and she'd ended up Googling the answers. Luckily the latest query was easy.

"I don't know. Maybe a lot more."

"Then I guess I'll just have to say yes, we can have pizza. And before you ask…yes to the extra cheese. Are we good?"

Her heart tightened in her chest as Alex gave her a high-five and then did a fist pump. She could only hope it would always be this easy to make her beautiful son happy. His tears tore her apart and made her wish she could shield him from the slings and arrows of the world, both real and imagined.

"You can help Doris paint the walls of the hallway," Mika said, handing her son a paintbrush. "The walls only. Not Doris. Not the floor. Not anything else. Got it?"

Alex scampered off with a promise to behave over his shoulder but she knew he'd be covered head to toe with black paint next time she saw him. He couldn't eat a slice of pizza without a portion of it ending up on his shirt, so she didn't have much hope that the paint would stay on the brush and the wall.

"He looks like you a little bit."

The deep voice cut through the silence and made her heart skip a beat.

Caleb.

She'd known he was going to help out but somehow she'd managed to not think about the fact that she would have to see him day in and day out. She called on every ounce of control to keep her features serene, as if seeing him didn't still hurt.

"Hello, Cal. Are you here to help? I have a list of things for you and your father."

She sounded calm, which frankly stunned the hell out of her because she sure didn't feel that way. Seeing him standing there not two feet in front of her was almost more than she could handle.

It was different today than on Sunday when she'd seen him in the diner. Now he was close enough that she could feel the heat from his skin and smell the clean scent of his soap. Cal didn't wear aftershave because it made him break out. Funny the things she could remember.

Cal placed his tool chest on the table and peered at the plans lying next to it. "Is this what you're building this year? It looks ambitious."

She had to bite back a retort that he would know all about ambition. Instead she nodded and reached for a soda in the cooler at her feet so she wouldn't have to look into his eyes. Ice blue and fringed with long, dark lashes, she'd been fascinated with them when they'd dated. She remembered how soft they could look when he was happy and how they turned almost gray when he wasn't.

Those eyes were studying the drawings, not giving her a second glance. She hated that it bothered her that he was so unaffected by this meeting, but then that was Cal. Grace under pressure or something like it. He didn't sweat the small stuff and she was absolutely positive that's where she fell in his life these days. Small and insignificant. After all, he'd left Applewood without a backward glance at the woman he'd supposedly loved.

Wait. That wasn't fair. She'd done her share of leaving as well.

"You know how it is. Every year we need to make it bigger and better. Something special to bring in people from Virginia Beach and beyond."

The nearest large city was Virginia Beach about forty-five minutes away. Applewood couldn't have made this haunted house for charity work if it didn't draw in customers from all over. In the last five years the Autumn Festival had grown by leaps and bounds.

"This should do it. What's the theme this year?"

Maybe she could do this after all. If they kept the conversation light and never actually looked each other in the eye.

"Victorian. Doris wanted to do clowns but…"

Mika shuddered at the thought.

Cal chuckled softly and this time did look up, their gazes colliding and sending her pulse racing. "I can imagine you were against it."

"There's nothing scarier than a clown," Mika declared, her mouth curled into a grimace. "I'd have to be in therapy for the next five years if we did that."

"Clowns don't bother me but I'm not fond of psychopathic

masked killers."

The strangeness of this moment wasn't lost on Mika. All that had happened between them and they were talking about what was scarier—a clown or a serial killer.

"Both are what nightmares are made of." She needed to bring this conversation to a halt. He'd stepped so close that there was only a few inches between his body and hers. "If you're ready to get to work I have a long list of jobs. Is your father coming later?"

Cal straightened and sighed, his hand rubbing the back of his neck. "He's staying with Mom. She said she wasn't feeling well. They told me to come on over here once school was out for the day."

Did he remember that she taught history at the high school? They'd started dating after he'd asked her to tutor him on the Renaissance. He'd later admitted that he didn't need the help; he just wanted to spend time with her. She'd found his confession incredibly sweet and endearing and it had made her fall in love with him even more deeply that day.

She picked up the list of woodworking projects from the table and held it out, careful not to let their fingers brush when he reached for it. "You can start anywhere on this. There are sketches in that folder but if you have a better idea for one of the props we're certainly open to it."

She was proud that her hand hadn't trembled but she still tucked it behind her, not wanting to take any chances. The sooner this exchange ended the better.

Cal scanned the list and nodded agreeably. "Doesn't look like anything too difficult, although I'm pretty rusty with the tools. I haven't made anything in a long time. If I have any trouble I can ask Dad for advice."

Cal and his father had always been close. They'd worked together every Sunday afternoon in Abe's woodshop building furniture and just hanging out.

Reaching for the folder of sketches, Cal stepped away and Mika could finally take a deep breath. With shaking fingers she tucked a stray strand of hair behind her ear, the emotion of this meeting finally unraveling her cool facade.

He tucked the list and a sketch under his arm and reached for his tool chest. "I'll start in the dungeon. Looks like there's plenty to do there. I'll let you know if I have any questions."

No, don't talk to me. Don't come near me anymore.

She watched his retreating figure, imposing even in this large warehouse space. Some urge she couldn't control and didn't expect made her call out to him.

"Alex doesn't look like me. He looks like Sarah."

Cal stopped but didn't turn around. He held himself stiffly, his spine ramrod straight and for a moment she thought she'd angered him somehow. Maybe that's what she'd meant to do. Get a reaction from him by talking about the past and her decision to stay and help her sister. Any reaction would do.

"No, honey. He looks like you too. His smile is yours. I could have picked him out of a crowd he looks so much like you."

Cal's voice was soft without a trace of impatience or fury. Her throat had tightened painfully and she had to swallow hard to be able to speak.

"He has Sarah's hair color and nose and his father's eyes."

Alex's father had died in a roadside bombing in Iraq without even knowing Sarah was pregnant.

"I suppose so. But he's yours, Michaela."

She nodded her head but he didn't see. He was already striding out of the room, leaving her standing there like the prize idiot she was. Cal was back in her life at least in this small way. She'd see him and talk to him. They might even laugh about something if it was truly funny.

He woke up parts of her that she'd shut down years ago. Memories of being young and in love, so idealistic.

So naive.

It was going to be a very long three months.

✦　✦　✦

CAL SWUNG THE hammer down on the nail harder than necessary but the physical outlet was just what his emotional state needed. He'd finally talked to Michaela and it hadn't gone all that badly.

It hadn't gone all that well either.

Seeing her son Alex had shaken Cal to the core and made it hard to think clearly. No matter what she said Alex looked like her. When Cal had seen the young boy he'd known it was her son immediately.

They'd talked about children so many times. Hand in hand as they'd swung on the back porch swing at her parents' house, they'd made plans about their life together. Now that he looked back those plans had never jived. He'd talk about traveling and all the places they would see and she would talk about their life in Applewood in between trips.

Then Sarah had gotten sick and nothing was ever the same. He didn't blame Mika's sister; hell, she'd been a young woman facing a grim prognosis and Cal had supported Mika's decision to care for her sister.

So they'd humored each other, the months stretching into years, neither one of them planning to give in on their vision of the future. It would have been comical if it hadn't been so damn painful and sad. They'd been doomed from the very start. Never had a chance.

"What are you building?"

Cal paused, his arm in the air ready to take another swing before setting the hammer down onto the sawhorse, his hand shaking slightly. When he'd vowed to keep his distance from Michaela he hadn't taken into consideration that he might want to do the same with Alex.

Turning around, Cal grabbed a towel and mopped at his sweaty brow. It was still warm this time of year and the warehouse wasn't air conditioned.

"A picture frame for one of those spooky paintings Doris makes."

The boy took a few steps forward and studied Cal's handiwork. "That's pretty cool. Where'd you learn to make stuff?"

Cal ran the towel on his damp neck before answering. "My dad. I think you know him. Abe Faulkner."

Alex nodded and then reached out his hand to run his fingers along the wood frame. "My mom can play guitar. She taught me a little."

"She's really good. She can play the piano too."

Alex looked up, his eyes wide. "Do you know my mom?"

Swallowing hard, Cal nodded. "I do. She and I were best friends all through our school years and beyond. Do you have a best friend?"

"Kenny," Alex replied. "Kenny Williams. He's better than me at baseball but I'm better at math."

"That's okay. You can help him and he can help you. Your mom helped me with my history homework and I showed her how to fish."

Alex looked down at the picture frame again. "Will you teach me how to do this? I promise I won't get in the way. My mom thinks I'm going to get hurt."

Michaela had always been the type to worry herself into a frazzle. But doing this was a bad idea for several completely different reasons.

"I'm not sure—"

"Please," Alex broke in, his tone pleading. "I won't be any trouble, I promise. Cross my heart."

Cal sighed in defeat and scratched at his chin, stubbly at the end of the day. The little boy's features were too much like hers and he felt that old familiar weakness he well remembered.

"Maybe," he conceded, and then had another idea that might make things less awkward. "Maybe I could teach you and your friend Kenny. That way you could help each other. You can be my apprentices."

If he worked with both kids it wouldn't be like he was doing something for Alex because he was Michaela's son.

It wouldn't be so...*personal.*

Alex ran toward the entrance to the hallway, his cheeks pink with excitement. "I'm going to go talk to Kenny. This is so cool.

Thank you, Mr. Faulkner."

"I think you better call me Cal if we're going to work together."

A wide grin and the boy was gone. Presumably to talk to
Kenny. And maybe his mom.

Which was going to open up a huge can of worms.

Cal had tried to avoid Michaela but the universe was against
him. Perhaps it was time to cleanse their souls and admit their
mistakes. It couldn't be any worse than the awkward conversation they'd had earlier, the tension thick and painful.

Now Cal understood what his father had been talking about.

It was time to talk to Michaela.

Chapter Four

"H E SAID I could help him and he would teach me and Kenny."

Alex was practically bouncing with excitement and Mika had to calm him down and repeat what he'd said one more time. With the typical eye roll she'd come to expect, her son took a deep breath and explained that Cal had agreed to teach him and Kenny how to do some woodwork. Somewhere in the rushed words she'd also learned that Cal had told Alex that he knew her and that they'd been best friends.

How in the hell was she supposed to say no to this?

"Sweetheart," she began, not wanting to see the excitement on his face disappear but needing him to understand that spending time with Cal wasn't the best idea. "Mr. Faulkner is a very busy man with a great deal of work to do. I can't have you bothering him."

Alex's brows pulled together and his smile drooped. "He said it would be okay. I won't be in his way. He said so."

"You or Kenny might get hurt."

Cal had done this. Put her in the untenable position of looking like the bad guy while he walked around still the local hero.

He didn't have any children and he didn't understand.

"I'll think about this," Mika finally said, her tone keeping Alex from arguing. The little boy's lips snapped shut and his expression turned stormy. He knew his chances were slim. "I will also talk to Mr. Faulkner about it and see what he has in mind."

Alex kicked at the table leg, his lower lip protruding. "You're gonna say no, aren't you?"

"If you sulk like that? Absolutely. Act like a big boy and I'll treat you that way. Now put that lower lip back before a little birdie perches on it and builds a nest."

Her teasing wrangled a smile from her son and she patted him on the back and pressed a kiss to his forehead. "Give me five minutes to get my things together and then we'll go get pizza. Why don't you go say goodbye to Doris?"

Alex skipped off and passed Cal coming the other way, his toolbox in his hand, looking exhausted. Hardening her heart, she stood up a little straighter and crossed her arms over her chest.

"What do you think you're doing, Cal? You should have talked to me first."

✦   ✦   ✦

MICHAELA'S CHEEKS WERE red with anger and he couldn't say he blamed her. The whole situation wasn't ideal but he'd been unable to turn Alex down. He held up his hands in a sign of surrender.

"Mea culpa, Mika. I should have talked to you first but he kind of cornered me. How do you say no when he looks up at you with those puppy dog eyes? Shit, I didn't want him to cry or something."

She huffed and began to roll up the sketches, her lips pressed together in a thin line. "I'm the mom and sometimes that means doing things that don't make me popular. This has put me in a difficult situation. Can't you see that?"

Cal placed his toolbox on the table and leaned forward so he could see her pissed off expression. She'd always had a head of steam but it usually didn't last too long.

"I can see your point. But let me ask you a question... Are you upset because you don't want me to spend time with Alex? Or are you upset because you don't want to spend time with me?"

Mika opened her mouth to answer and then snapped it shut. Her hands were visibly shaking and he felt a twist in his gut that he was the cause. He'd meant it when he told his father that he didn't want her to be stressed and hurt by his presence. It was time they hashed out all the pain and recriminations and moved on with their lives.

"This is not about me. This is about a little boy. All I need is for him to get attached to you and then you leave. He's had enough of that in his life."

She'd wrapped her arms around her torso as if she needed protection from him. Some kind of shield to keep him at arm's length. She didn't need it. Their past was barrier enough.

"I'm not trying to hurt your son, Mika. He started talking to me."

"He's curious about a lot of things but I don't indulge him when he wants to play with matches or knives."

Her anger was already starting to abate, never able to hold a grudge. She'd been grasping at straws anyway in her attempt to paint him as the villain.

"I'll gladly take my share of the blame here, Mika. Most of it, in fact. But not all."

Her fingers curled around her large leather purse as she stuffed the sketches inside. "You make me so angry I can't think straight. I'm normally the most placid person anyone could ever know but a few minutes in your company and I'm a total bitch. I don't think it's healthy, honestly."

Placid? Since when could Michaela Adams be called *placid* of all things? She'd been a firecracker with a snarky mouth when he'd known her.

"Why would you even want to be called that insipid word? Hell, that's not the woman I knew. The Michaela I loved had fire and passion. She cared about people and causes. She was brave and strong. She sure as shit wasn't placid."

"I am strong. I've just grown up—something you might want to try. My life isn't about just me anymore. Unlike you."

Another dig at his solitary lifestyle. He wasn't going to bite. Not tonight.

"I'm tired of arguing with you. We never get anywhere and simply run laps, saying the same things over and over. When you're ready to have an honest talk about the past let me know. Until then I'll keep to myself. I'll let you tell Alex that I can't spend time with him. Just blame it on me."

"I wouldn't do that," she denied, her shoulders stiffening. "I know how he can manipulate things to get his own way so I don't blame you. I'll talk to him."

"You'll talk to him but you won't talk to me." Cal lifted his toolbox from the table and headed for the door. "This was part of our problem."

She looked like she wanted to toss something at him but instead she let him walk out of the door without a word. He tossed his tools into the back of his truck and pulled out of the parking lot, pointing the vehicle toward his temporary home.

Cal hadn't wanted to do this volunteer job for this very reason. Tension. Animosity. Pure anger.

All those bad feelings were held deep inside, pushed down, ignored, and left to fester for way too long.

It was only a matter of time before everything blew up in one glorious technicolor explosion.

Chapter Five

MIKA SLID A slice of pizza onto a plate and handed it to Charlotte. Alex was in bed and they were relaxing in front of a chick flick and looking forward to the weekend. It had been a long week and seeing Cal every day at the haunted house site hadn't made it go any faster. They'd managed to be polite to one another but it had been a struggle.

"I just think you should cut him some slack, that's all." Charlotte picked off a piece of sausage and popped it into her mouth. "For all the crap he's done you're no angel in this either. You both are stubborn as mules and have held onto the past way too long. Let it go and move on. I think Cal's a nice guy."

Apparently everyone did. His return had set the gossip mills buzzing and the young single women into a collective swoon. Mika seemed to be the only one who wasn't as welcoming.

"He still makes me mad. He blows into town and turns everything on its ear and then he's just going to walk away again." Mika blew out a breath as she recalled their conversation last week. She'd been fuming about it for days. "He made fun of me for saying I was placid."

"Good. Since Cal left you've been slowly fading away. You're not the girl you used to be."

"I've grown up," Mika protested. "That's what people are supposed to do."

"Grow up, but don't become old before your time. There's a difference." Charlotte sipped at her wine before grimacing slightly. "By the way, I told Cal it was okay for him to spend some time with Kenny teaching him woodwork."

Mika slapped the slice of pizza back down on the plate. "Are you serious? After I told Alex he couldn't and chewed Cal a new one for saying he would? Is everybody out to make me the bad guy here?"

Charlotte's brows went up and she cocked her head to the side. "Are you being the bad guy? Give me one good reason not to let Cal teach Alex some woodworking skills. A reason other than you two broke up and you're still butthurt. That's not a good reason."

Mika started to answer, filled with righteous indignation, but the hilarity of the situation wasn't lost on her and she began to giggle. At first softly and then loudly when Charlotte joined in.

"Butthurt. That word always cracks me up. Yes, I guess I am butthurt. And bitchy. And stubborn. I'm not sure why you put up with me, honestly."

"Because I love you," Charlotte answered promptly. "And you love me. Even when we do things that don't make sense. And Mika? This attitude you have toward Cal doesn't make sense. He didn't leave you—you left each other. You couldn't move to Chicago and he couldn't stay here. I bet you broke his heart."

"I doubt he stayed celibate in my honor." Mika rolled her

eyes imagining all the sophisticated women from the city that Cal had dated and bedded. Dressed to the nines, their hair and makeup perfect, they would complement his dark good looks at the theatre or a fancy restaurant. Scowling at her short, unpainted nails, she could never compete with glamour like that. She was a mom first and foremost and then a teacher. Expensive clothes and jewels were not a requirement.

She sounded defensive and she didn't mean to. Her decision to adopt Alex and become his mother had been the absolute right one.

"Cal is a good man." Charlotte reached out and patted Mika's hand. "You told him to go, Mika. You told him to go on to Chicago and that you would follow. You didn't. You strung Cal along for over a year and stayed here in the end. If anyone has a reason to be bitter...well, it isn't you."

"He could have come back," Mika whispered, her heart hurting at the memory that still had such power over her emotions. "For the longest time I kept hoping he would."

Charlotte shook her head and sighed. "He couldn't come back. You both took sledgehammers to each other's hearts. Neither of you hold the moral high ground here. Maybe it's time to forgive each other and start again."

Her friend was actually serious. "Start again? Are you suggesting that Cal and I date or something? That's absurd."

"I wasn't suggesting any such thing but obviously you're thinking about it." Charlotte wore a delighted expression. "I was just saying you could pretend you were meeting him for the very first time. But if you want to ask him out then by all means go for it. I bet he'd say yes."

That was scarier than anything.

✦   ✦   ✦

A POKER GAME with Jon and his friends seemed like a great way for Cal to spend Friday night. It had been a long, tension-filled week with Mika and he needed the break. She'd been frosty when he'd tried to engage her in conversation and honestly he was exhausted. He'd tried to put the past behind them and stay in the present but she wasn't cooperating.

Jon's condo in Virginia Beach was the typical bachelor pad, sparsely decorated except for photos of him and his girlfriend Ali. He probably spent most of his time at her place by the looks of things.

The group was gathered in the kitchen taking a break and diving into the boxes of pizza that had just been delivered. Cal bit into a slice before knocking back a shot of whiskey, feeling the burn all the way to his gut.

It was exactly what he'd needed to relax and unwind.

Zane, Rick, and Chris were laidback and didn't mind losing a few bucks in a card game so they were a-okay with Cal, although it was clear he was the odd man out. The four men knew each other so well from their years as active duty SEALs they barely had to even speak to each other. It reminded Cal of how it had been during those early years in the FBI when camaraderie had been more important than politics.

Jon slapped Cal on the back and refilled his whiskey glass. "How are you getting settled in? It's got to be a real culture shock going from Chicago to a little town like Applewood."

Cal didn't gulp the amber colored liquid this time, sipping at it instead. Jon had offered to let him spend the night if he had a few too many but he'd rather sleep in his own bed.

"It's going fine but yes, it is a change. Applewood rolls up the streets about nine o'clock on the weekends and nobody locks their door. I'd forgotten any place could be like that."

Danger had become second nature to Cal these last several years, always looking over his shoulder. He was only now beginning to lose the paranoia that accompanied deep undercover work. It had kept him alive but now he had no need of it.

"You got a love a place like that," Rick chuckled, grabbing another slice of pizza. "The world is a dangerous place and yet they have no idea. I hope they can hold onto that innocence awhile longer."

"Me too, although I'm not sure how much longer I'll be there. Mom's feeling better every day and honestly Dad should just retire and close shop."

Jon frowned. "If you didn't stay would you go back to Chicago?"

Cal wasn't sure there was anything to go back to. He hadn't heard a word about the internal investigation into his handling of the Alan Morton case, which probably meant they were planning to hang him from the highest tree. Cal hadn't done a damn thing wrong but powerful people weren't going to let this rest.

"Maybe." Shrugging, Cal leaned against the kitchen counter. "I don't think I'm wanted very much in Applewood. It might be better if I just left when my lease is up."

"You're not wanted by everyone or you're not wanted by Michaela?" Jon asked. The other men had wandered onto the back deck, leaving Cal and Jon alone in the kitchen. "I take it from your expression that the reunion didn't go well."

"You could say that," Cal snorted. "She raked me over the coals and even told me not to spend time with her son. All in all it was a failure of epic proportions. We need to clear the air but I don't really know how to make that happen. Communicating with females has never been my strong suit."

"I wouldn't say it's mine either." Jon scratched his chin in thought. "Have you thought about getting her alone and not letting her leave until she yells it all out? Let her call you all sorts of names until she's run out of steam."

"It's crossed my mind but I'm not sure that even then she won't be mad. She blames me for the demise of our relationship. Hell, maybe she's right. I've made mistakes in my life and this is probably just one more."

"Is it your fault?"

Cal had spent the better part of the week pondering that very question.

"I don't know," he admitted. "I think we both had a hand in it but I guess she could make a case that it was my doing."

"So apologize. Take all the damn blame. Grovel a little. Then you can't say you didn't pull out all the stops to make this right. If she still can't put the past behind her…well…you did all you could and it's her problem now."

Maybe that's what had been holding Cal back all this week. If he confronted Mika and pushed her to talk about the past and she couldn't move on then there was no hope for them.

Ever.

He wasn't sure if he could close the book on Mika and everything she represented so completely.

At one time in his life she'd been everything.

He'd been happy then.

What was he now?

Chapter Six

"IT WAS AWESOME, Mom. Kenny and I made picture frames for the haunted house."

It was a week later at the worksite and Mika was looking forward to a hot bath and a glass of wine. Between being a mother, a teacher, and one of the festival coordinators she was officially exhausted. She'd been here every night of the week along with Cal and the awkwardness between the two of them had only grown, stretching her nerves to their breaking point.

Of course Alex and Kenny weren't tired in the least. Both of them were practically walking on air—or strutting might be a better description. The male gene that liked to hammer at things had been well satisfied this evening and the boys along with Cal looked none the worse for wear. Mika had to admit that Charlotte had been right. Letting the boys spend some time with Cal wasn't the worst thing in the world.

It only felt that way to her.

Charlotte reached down and gave Kenny a big hug. "Daddy's waiting at home for us so we need to skedaddle. Now what do you say to Mr. Faulkner?"

Kenny turned and grinned. "Thank you! When can we do

this again?"

"Kenny," Charlotte admonished but Cal just smiled indulgently.

"Anytime. You and Alex were good helpers and there's plenty of work to be done. Next time we'll sand and stain what you've done so wear old clothes."

Charlotte corralled her son and headed for the door. "It's been a long week and I feel like I could sleep for days. I don't know where you get your energy, Cal."

"Good clean living."

Mika rolled her eyes at his teasing words. She hadn't spent time with him these last years but she highly doubted that was the case.

"Mom, can Alex spend the night?" Kenny asked. "Please? He hasn't spent the night in a really long time."

Four or five weeks wasn't all that long but in a young child's life it felt like a lifetime Mika supposed.

"Can I, Mom? Please?" Alex pleaded, knowing full well how she folded like a cheap tent when he looked so adorable.

Charlotte laughed and shrugged her shoulders. "It's okay with me if it's okay with you."

"I suppose, but promise me you'll be good."

"Yes!"

Both Alex and Kenny celebrated with a high five and then Charlotte herded them out of the door with a wave. "See you tomorrow!"

Charlotte's exit left just Mika and Cal standing in the parlor area. Silently she began to pack up her things, not sure what to say after eating crow about Alex. To her surprise he hadn't bragged about her capitulation, simply nodding and thanking her for thinking it over and giving him a chance.

A chance? Was that what this was?

"I hope you were able to get some work done tonight and that the boys weren't too much trouble."

She shoved a half empty water bottle into her oversized bag, hating that her voice sounded shaky. She didn't want to be as affected by him as she clearly was. Just his nearness was enough to make her nervous.

"They were fine." His voice was deep and soft and her stomach twisted in her abdomen as she remembered him saying much more personal things in her ear during intimate moments. "They're really good kids. You've done a good job, Mika. You should be proud of yourself."

Parenthood wasn't awash with opportunities for praise and she didn't fight the warm glow that took up residence near her heart. She tried so hard to be a good mother to Alex but she wasn't always sure she succeeded.

"Thank you, Cal." She slung her purse over her shoulder, her fingers tight around the soft leather. "I guess I'll see you Monday night."

She didn't even get to the door before he stepped into her path. "Wait. I think it's time for us to talk, don't you? Really talk, Mika. Get everything out into the open at last."

That was the last thing she wanted to do. His presence these last weeks had taken her out of her comfort zone and she hadn't had a decent night's sleep since.

"I really need to get home–"

"Stop, Mika." Cal placed his hand on her shoulder and his

touch felt electrified. It had been too long. Much too long. "Please. We can't go on like this. I have some things I want to say and I think you do too."

Her chest felt tight and her stomach tumbled and churned. She hadn't realized how much she'd repressed her emotions until Cal had come back and dug up the past.

"I can't think why this is a good idea."

Cal squeezed her shoulder, a half-smile on his lips. "Walking on eggshells around each other isn't going to make this any easier. I'll let you yell at me all you want—how does that sound?"

She was past that. At least she thought she was. But she wasn't sure she could keep up a serene facade in front of others.

"If people see us together…"

"I get where you're going with this, although I don't give a shit what anyone thinks. How about I pick up some takeout and we go down to the lake and talk? Unless things have changed no one will bother us there."

The lake had been their "special place" and it brought back too many memories that she'd rather not dwell on.

"No, how about we just eat here?" No one would question this as they already knew he had volunteered. "I can run down the block and pick up something."

"I'll do it. You just relax. You look like you're dead on your feet. Do you ever sleep?"

Cal didn't wait for her answer. He'd already pulled open the front door and stepped into the darkness before she could protest.

Now that he'd left she could make a run for it of course, but she knew him well enough to know he'd just follow her to her house. She could clam up and let him talk without saying a word. Not letting him know how much he'd hurt her. How often she still thought about him in those few moments of quiet she had after Alex went to sleep.

Or she could finally tell him that he'd broken her heart in a million pieces and she'd never been able to glue it back together again. He'd ruined her for any other man and she hated him for that.

Shutting the door behind him, Mika leaned against it and felt the sting of tears prick her eyes. She had no idea how to deal with this or what to say. She only knew that being this close to him wasn't a good idea.

She couldn't allow herself to fall in love with him again. She wouldn't survive it this time.

CAL SWALLOWED THE last bite of cheeseburger and tossed his crumpled napkin into the styrofoam container. Currently ensconced on one of the old velvet couches in the parlor area, they'd eaten in mostly companionable silence broken only by a few innocuous questions here and there. Mostly reflections on past haunted houses and Halloweens or maybe the weather this time of year and how it compared to last year.

They were circling each other like a couple of boxers in the ring but no one wanted to throw the first punch.

Reaching across, Cal pilfered a fry from the still large stack and added insult to injury by dipping into her well of ketchup before popping it into his mouth. Her mouth fell open in shock and he couldn't contain a bit of evil laughter to top off his stunt. If that didn't get her talking nothing would.

"I can't believe you stole one of my fries." Her pretty face was screwed up into a frown. "Eat your own."

"I did," he laughed easily. "And they're all gone. But I'm still hungry and you've barely touched yours. Are you not hungry?"

Mika's cheeks flushed a lovely pink and he could tell he was the reason she was too nervous to eat.

Good. She wasn't unaffected. That was something anyway.

"I ate quite a bit actually." Mika pointed the half-eaten cheeseburger. "Maybe I'm saving room for dessert."

Cal chuckled and reached into the brown bag, pulling out a gigantic slab of chocolate cake. It was her favorite.

"You mean this? I bought this for me."

He couldn't even keep a straight face while he said it but she scowled in mock anger just to tease him right back.

"There better be two forks in there, buster, or this could get messy."

He reached into the bag again and then held them up in triumph. "Relax, missy. There are two. There's enough fudge cake here for three or four people."

She plucked the plastic fork from his hand. "Or two hungry ones. I love Julie's chocolate cake. It's the best in the county."

She took a big bite, her eyes closed in ecstasy. There was no better time to piss her off than right now.

"So we need to talk about the past. We need to make our peace."

Her lids snapped open and her mouth tightened. "I know you think we should do this but I think it might be a mistake.

What point is there after all these years?"

"Because you're still angry with me. I'll take the blame, Mika. I can see why you would hate me and I understand why it's difficult to have me around now. But please understand that back then I didn't think I had any choice."

The happiness that she'd radiated only moments before was gone and she tapped her fork against her thigh, obviously trying to find the right words to express how little she thought of him.

"It's not all your fault," she whispered, her head dipping down so she was staring at the cake. "For a long time I thought it was or maybe just hoped it, but Charlotte talked some sense into me last night. I know that we both screwed up. But it was easier after you left to just blame you and make you out to be the bad guy."

"I did the same thing," Cal offered, still not convinced she didn't want to see him drawn and quartered. The last time he'd been in Applewood there had been so much fury and hurt in her eyes when she looked at him. "I kept telling myself that you were never sincere about moving to Chicago to be with me, that you never wanted me to succeed. It was easier than admitting that I was being selfish while you were being altruistic."

Mika lifted her head, a snort on her lips. "I'm no saint, Cal, so don't paint me into that corner. I stayed with Sarah while she was sick because she was my sister and I loved her. And when she died I took over caring for Alex. It wasn't charity. It was what any decent family member would do for another."

"Not everyone would have done what you did," he said gently. "Trust me, I've seen the lowest of the low in my job. What you did was selfless. You put aside your own life and happiness to do this amazing job. Now that I see Alex I know that you did the right thing. It wouldn't have been the same if you brought him to Chicago."

She'd promised to follow him there when Sarah passed on but then Alex had only been a baby. Her parents hadn't been in the best of health and caring for an infant was asking too much of them.

So she'd adopted him and decided that bringing him up in Applewood was the best thing. A place where she had a job and family and friends to give her all the support she needed with the challenge.

Her lips trembled and her face had gone pale. "Every day I thought about you. Every single damn day I wanted to come to Chicago. But it was never the right time. We were...I don't know...comfortable, I guess. It was simpler here. Alex was happy. My parents were happy."

Reaching out, he placed his hand over hers, the skin soft under his fingertips. How could he have forgotten how wonderful she felt?

"How about you? Were you happy?"

"I'm not unhappy, but honestly I stopped thinking about my own happiness a long time ago." Her lips were turned down at the corners and she looked so sad Cal had to steel himself from pulling her into his arms. "I put Alex first and I know that it was the right thing to do. But that doesn't mean that it didn't hurt. I thought about you...so many times. I don't want you to think it was easy for me. That's why I kept telling you I was coming to Chicago. I wanted to believe that I really could. That is the truth, but it only made you hate me. You thought I was stringing you along."

Cal had thought it and hearing her now made him ashamed that he'd ever believed she'd do something like that. He should have known that she was torn by her loyalty and love for her family and her love and desire for a future with him.

"I was a complete asshole and I'm sorry. Really sorry. I put you in an impossible position and I didn't see it at the time."

"What about you, Cal? Were you happy?" Their fingers tangled together and the warmth from her skin penetrated straight to his bones. "For the longest time I didn't want you to be but now I truly hope you have been. I want you to have a good life. While mine hasn't been perfect it's been good."

Rubbing his jaw, Cal let out a bark of laughter. "That's a good question. One I'm not sure I know how to answer. There have been happy times. There have also been times in my life that I wouldn't want to repeat for anything in the world. Doing this job...being undercover for months or years...living a lie twenty-four seven does things to you. You can lose yourself so easily. Sometimes I wonder if I even know who I am anymore. All I know is that I was caught up in the political games and the competition. Bringing in the bad guys wasn't the point any longer. Winning was everything."

"And now?"

"I'm pretty sure I've lost." Cal hadn't heard from his superiors in weeks. "They'll probably ask me to resign so they don't have to fire me. It's over for me there."

"How can they do that? What happened?"

Cal took a long drink from his water bottle, drawing out the moment until he had some semblance of an answer. He'd put a great deal of thought into that very question.

"I was the lead on an investigation into organized crime. It took me about three years but I fought my way up the ladder until I was head of a gambling and prostitution syndicate in Chicago. I took down some big names. One night I took down a guy named Alan Morton. He was one sick bastard so please don't feel sorry for him. Anyway, he had a lot of friends in high places and they had Washington D.C. connections. Long story short? They screamed until they got what they wanted. My ass on a platter."

"That's horrible that they can do that. You don't have any recourse?"

She was genuinely upset for him but he'd made some peace with his destiny. He wasn't completely there but he'd given up on false hope.

"Sure, I could get a lawyer and drag this out for years. They'd hold hearings and take statements but in the end nothing would change. My career and my reputation would be in tatters. At least this way if I leave quietly I'll get to keep some of the respect I've worked so hard to earn. The people who really know me won't buy into the bullshit."

There were only a few, actually. His job wasn't conducive to building close friendships.

"I know you didn't do anything wrong."

There wasn't a smidge of doubt in her voice, although she knew little about his work and less about how shallow his life had become since he'd left her.

"You can't possibly know that. Maybe I'm a terrible agent or an awful person."

"No." Mika shook her head, color in her cheeks. "I know. You were always the one to make sure everything was just right. In school. Playing football. Even when you were making a piece of furniture there were no shortcuts. You couldn't have changed that much in eight years."

"For someone that hates me you're being kind of nice."

"I don't hate you." Her voice was a whisper and he had to lean down to hear her. "I tried and sometimes I succeeded, but right now I don't hate you. How can I when you offered to take all the blame?"

Cal chuckled and wrapped both of his hands around hers. "I have to be honest and admit that wasn't my idea. A friend of mine suggested I do that. But once I thought about it I realized that it really was my fault. I should have come back to help you. I should have–"

"Stop." Mika pulled her hand away and made a cutting motion in the air. "You were just out of the military and trying to make a career for yourself. You needed the money to help your parents since the economy sucked. And if I'm being really honest here? I kept thinking you'd come back. That you'd hate Chicago as much as I did and you'd come back here to me. But Applewood was never big enough for your dreams, was it? I understand that now when I think about what I want for Alex. When he's grown I can't hold him here because of my wants and needs. It wouldn't be fair, and I wasn't fair to you."

"So what I'm taking from this conversation is that we're both a pair of selfish jerks who should have done things differently. Except we can't go back in time and change any of it. We only have the here and now."

Mika's lips drooped and her eyes glistened with tears. "You're right. We can't go back. We had our chance and we blew it. Now we're two different people with grown-up responsibilities. But I'm still glad we talked about this. I didn't want to but as usual you knew best."

Mika tugged her hand away and stood, quickly walking across the room to where her bag sat on the table. Cal levered up from the couch, an uneasy feeling deep in his gut. If this was closure he didn't like it one bit.

"What are you doing? There's still chocolate cake left."

Slinging her purse on her shoulder Mika smiled sadly. "I'm leaving. Can you lock up the warehouse behind me?"

Cal took a few steps toward her but she moved back as if to ward him off. "I can but I guess I don't understand. Why are you going? I thought we were making progress here."

"We are. We did. But we've said everything there is to say, don't you think?"

They'd beaten the dead horse of who was to blame, that was for sure, but it didn't feel *finished* to Cal. It hadn't ever felt that way and hadn't he always known that deep down? That's why he'd been terrified to come here and at the same time he couldn't stay away. He wanted to be near her even though it hurt like hell.

"It's not over. We're not done," he growled, moving swiftly to cover the short distance between them. Before she could protest or push him away he'd gathered her in his arms, pressing her soft curves against every inch of himself. Nothing had felt this good since he'd left this damn town. "We still have this."

This was a kiss that splintered his soul into tiny slivers that pierced his already aching heart. He hadn't known what had been missing in his life until this very moment.

His Michaela.

He'd been treading water, existing but not really living when they'd been apart. He'd pretended everything was fine, but hearing her say they had nothing between them anymore had finally pulled his head out of his ass. This couldn't be the final page in their story. There was so much more if she'd just open herself up to the possibility.

Was it too late?

His lips slid over hers, seeking the answer even as her hands crept up his arms and wound around his neck. She tasted of chocolate and of something else... That essence he hadn't found anywhere with anyone.

She tasted of forever.

As suddenly as the kiss had begun it was over, her hands pushing at his chest. He instantly stepped back, knowing that what he wanted was going to be a hard sell. All that stubbornness was still there and something about him brought it out of her in spades.

Her eyes were wide and she was visibly trembling. He reached out to steady her but she shook her head and stepped away to press her palm to the table for support. Neither of them spoke for a moment, the tension and anguish between them palpable.

"Don't do that again."

Her voice was as shaky as her hands but she looked him right in the eyes when she said it. Without another word she practically sprinted to the front door, throwing it open so hard that it slammed into the wall behind it. She was gone into the night, leaving Cal standing there with warring emotions in his gut. Hope and despair brawling it out for supremacy.

He was sure of one thing after tonight. There was still something between them and she felt it too. It might not be enough. Hell, *he* might not be enough but he had to try.

Cal wanted Mika's love and a second chance. But he sure as hell didn't deserve it.

Chapter Seven

CAL SAT ON his parents' front porch the next day alongside his mother. They were enjoying the cool early morning weather with a cup of coffee and some fresh baked donuts he'd picked up at the diner on the way.

"I shouldn't be eating these." Alice Faulkner bit into the chocolate frosted with a sigh of contentment. "But you're a good son for bringing them. I guess if I don't eat sweets too often it's not so bad."

"I'm a lousy son but thank you. I had a hankering for them this morning and I thought you might like some too."

He'd barely slept last night after everything that happened with Mika. His mind had whirled with images of the past and possibilities for their future. Should they have one, that is. He knew she still had feelings but he wasn't convinced that deep down she didn't blame him for all that had happened.

"Who told you that?" Alice scolded gently. "You are a good son. My favorite son."

He was her only child unless she was living a secret life no one knew anything about.

"I rarely came home. I should have and I didn't."

"You were building your life and career. You're supposed to do that and we didn't expect anything different."

"And now I have nothing to show for it."

Cal couldn't keep the bitterness from seeping into his tone. All the years of hard work were down the drain.

"Maybe you concentrated on the wrong things."

Pouring himself another cup of coffee, Cal pondered his mother's observation. She hadn't asked many questions about his life in Chicago since he'd been back nor had she asked much about Mika.

"I was trying to make something of myself."

"You always were ambitious." She shook her head when he offered to refill her cup. "I admired that but I also hoped you'd take time out to find a good woman and have a family."

That was half a sentence.

"You mean you wished I had married Mika and settled down in Applewood."

His mother pursed her lips, her gaze far away. "I think you and Mika could have a good life but I'm sure there are other women as well you could be happy with. Maybe even happier. Mika is a lovely girl but she can be bull-headed and set in her ways. She certainly left you high and dry after you moved."

Cal started to defend Mika but then simply chuckled. Alice Faulkner wasn't fooling anybody. She adored Mika and always had.

"Are you trying out some reverse psychology, Mom? We both know that the breakup was just as much my fault as hers. If I'd been any kind of man I would have stayed here and helped her raise Alex but I cut and ran. I took the easy way out."

Alice's brows shot up in mock surprise. "I didn't realize your life had been so leisurely since you left. I must have missed that. How lucky for you."

"You know what I mean," Cal growled in frustration. "Maybe my life wasn't a bed of roses but the only person I had to be worried about was me. Hell, I don't even have any plants in my apartment to water and if I did they'd be dead. I probably shouldn't be trusted with an actual human being."

Yet for some strange reason Cal had taken to Alex right away. The boy needed a father and Mika needed…

Whoa.

What the hell was he thinking? He wasn't father or husband material. He was an agent who put the bad guys behind bars. It was the only thing he knew how to do and he was damn good at it.

"I'm not going to argue with you, son, but I think you have more love and care in you than you know. Just don't make the same mistake twice."

"Leaving Mika? Even if I stay there's no guarantee she wants a relationship with me. When I kissed her last–"

Cal broke off, heat rising in his cheeks. He hadn't meant to say anything about the kiss last night, least of all to his mother.

Alice Faulkner wore a pleased smile as she sipped her coffee. "A kiss? About time. I've been waiting weeks for that to happen. Did she kiss you back?"

He did not want to discuss this with her.

"Yes."

"So things are moving in the right direction. Excellent."

If his mother had rubbed her hands together with a maniacal

laugh he wouldn't have been surprised. He'd suspected all along that this "volunteer" thing was just a ruse to throw them together.

"It doesn't mean she wants me. In fact, she told me to never do it again and ran out. She hates me."

"She hates that you've made her feel something. That poor girl has lived for her son and that's fine but she needs something for herself. She needs to be loved."

"What makes you think I still love her?" Cal asked desperately, hopping to his feet. He paced the worn boards of the front porch, the paint cracking and chipping away. His father was too old to be thinking about taking care of this and Cal made a quick mental note to handle it himself. "That ship sailed long ago."

His mother plucked the last chocolate frosted from the bakery box. "Lying to yourself isn't going to help this situation. You still love her and she still loves you. Why do you think you both stayed single all these years? I know there have been other women, Cal. You haven't been a saint. Far from it, I'll bet."

"I worked sixteen hours a day and she was busy raising a child. That's why we're alone and not because of some deep unrequited love. After all these years that would be ridiculous."

Alice Faulkner slapped the donut down on a plate and looked him right in the eye, making him stop pacing and face her. She was a formidable woman at all times but when she was intense like this she was a force to be reckoned with.

"Look me in the eye and tell me you don't have feelings for Mika and I'll leave you alone." He didn't move a muscle, too confused about his feelings to make a denial but not sure he could call the swirling emotions that made him sick to his stomach love. "Go on, boy. Say it."

He couldn't and that was a problem. A big one.

He did love her. Now what in the hell was he going to do about it?

Chapter Eight

I T WAS A quiet Sunday morning. Mika and Alex were enjoying breakfast in their sunny kitchen decorated in yellow and white. She rested her chin in her hands as she watched Alex demolish a stack of pancakes, her own untouched. She'd barely slept the last two nights as she'd tossed and turned in her bed, playing the kiss with Cal over and over until she thought she'd scream with frustration.

It never should have happened and she'd be crazy to see something there that really wasn't. Cal was probably bored and at loose ends here in Applewood, and kissing his old girlfriend seemed like a good idea at the time. He wouldn't appreciate her building fantasies about love and forever based on a short kiss.

But there had been tongue.

He certainly hadn't lost any of his skill. Making love with Cal had been the pinnacle of ecstasy and no other man had ever measured up the few times she'd tried to eradicate him from her mind. In other words, he knew his way around a female's private parts. Especially hers, as she'd given him exclusive and unlimited access from the time they'd started dating to when they'd finally called it quits after his stint in the Navy and then joining the

FBI.

"Do you want more?"

She pushed her own plate toward her son but he shook his head and shoved another bite in his mouth.

"No. Is Kenny coming over to play this morning?"

There wasn't much left on the little boy's plate although there was plenty of maple syrup smeared across his face. Her heart lurched in her chest as he grinned, reminding her so much of Sarah. Perhaps of his father as well, although she'd never know.

Mika had never met Alex's father and Sarah had only spoken of him a few times.

"Yes, so you need to finish up your breakfast and pick up your toys."

Alex gave her a look that said Mika was crazy as it didn't make any sense to clean up toys that were only going to be dragged out again, but the mother part of her was always trying to press for order despite all the chaos.

"When do we get to help Cal again?"

Mika's fingers tightened on the warm coffee cup but she managed to keep her features neutral. Alex was too young to understand her inner turmoil when it came to Caleb Faulkner and it was her job to make sure the little boy didn't get hurt along the way. Cal hadn't said anything about staying in Apple-wood long term and already her son had a mighty big case of hero worship.

"Soon," she said noncommittally and then tried to change the subject. "What are you going to be for Halloween?"

It was still early but Halloween was second only to Christmas for Alex and he loved picking out his costume each year.

"I was thinking I would be a soldier. Or maybe a policeman. Did you know Cal was a soldier and a cop? Isn't that cool, Mom?"

"Very cool. What about the zombie costume you were eyeing in that catalog? I thought you wanted to be something scary."

"No way," Alex scoffed, giving her that look again that said she was as dumb as a stump. She distinctly remembered giving it to her parents as well. It was a rite of passage for a child to think they were much smarter than their parent. "I want to be a hero. I want to be someone who saves people."

"You've got time to figure it out. Maybe we can drive into Virginia Beach and you can look at the costumes there."

A quick knock on her front door told her Charlotte and Kenny had arrived. They'd long since dispatched with any ceremony so Charlotte pushed open the door with a wave. Alex scrambled down from his chair and the two boys scampered off into the backyard.

Mika sighed in resignation. The toys could be picked up later.

"Please tell me you have a full pot of coffee."

Charlotte sniffed the air appreciatively and reached into the cabinet, pulling down a mug.

"I do but you may have to wrestle me for it."

Charlotte poured herself a cup and settled in the chair Alex had just vacated. "You look like hell. Did you walk with the undead last night or something?"

Mika groaned and gulped down more of her coffee, the scorching liquid burning her tongue. "Thank you very much. I sure know where to go when I need a pick me up."

"I'm just calling it like I see it. Are you coming down with the flu?"

Mika's gaze flickered to the windows overlooking the backyard where the two boys were happily playing with a blue and red soccer ball. "I kissed Cal Friday night after you left."

Charlotte's eyes bugged and her mouth fell open, the coffee cup paused halfway to her lips. The expression would have been comical if anything else about the situation was in the least funny.

"Oh. My. God. Is that all you did? Are you back together? How was it? Did he tell you he still has feelings? Do you still have feelings? What a stupid question…of course you still have feelings. This is Cal we're talking about. He's a man among men. Oh my God, Mika."

Charlotte had said all that in one single breath and it showed. She gasped and sucked in air as if starved of oxygen, almost dropping her mug and spilling scalding hot coffee down her clothes.

"Just calm down." Mika held up her hands in surrender. She needed to talk about what had happened but clearly Charlotte had already made up her mind as to what Mika should do. "It was a kiss. Afterwards I told him he shouldn't do it again."

Charlotte looked scandalized. "Why the heck not? If a man like Cal wanted to kiss me I'd drape myself across his lap and let him have his wicked way with me."

Mika didn't want to think about all the times she'd done pretty much that very thing.

"There's too much…history between us. We talked Friday

night and pretty much had it out. Finally after all this time. He blamed himself. I blamed myself. We both realized we'd done stupid shit and then he kissed me. It probably didn't mean anything. He was probably just caught up in the nostalgia or something."

Except the kiss hadn't felt like before. There had been something new there. Cal was different now. More commanding. More in control. Someone she could trust and depend on. She could feel that he'd changed these last years, especially when he'd talked about losing his career. It had meant so much to him and her heart ached for his shattered dreams.

"Sure. Yeah. Nostalgia." Charlotte rolled her eyes and stuck out her tongue. "That's why I go around kissing people. Why, just the other day I laid a big one right on David Brown's lips just because he used to bring me potato chips when we were in junior high. I just felt so…nostalgic."

"Are you done now? Can we get back to my problem?"

Charlotte filched a piece of bacon off the tray on the counter. "Okay, I'll be serious. And seriously I don't see that you have a problem, my friend. Unless of course you don't find Cal attractive. Is that the real problem? You don't want him anymore?"

"My good sense is saying he's the last person I should want."

Charlotte waggled her eyebrows. "Does any other body part have an opinion?"

Mika had been single for so long she'd thought that perhaps her sex life was completely in the past. Something she thought about every now and then but nothing she would ever recapture.

"If you're referring to my girl parts, then yes they have an opinion, but I'm sure you can guess what it is."

Her expression turned sober and Charlotte leaned forward and placed her hand over Mika's in a comforting gesture. "And your heart?"

"It hurts," Mika admitted, closing her eyes for a moment and taking a deep breath to manage the ache centered directly in her chest. "I always told myself that he tossed my heart and love aside as if it was nothing. He was a bastard or worse. But he's not. Not really. As much as he hurt me I hurt him just as much."

Charlotte squeezed Mika's fingers. "Maybe this is your second chance."

"Do people really get those?" Mika pulled away and fell back into a kitchen chair, slumping in defeat. "Let's follow this to its logical conclusion, shall we? We kissed. So let's say I let him kiss me again. And again. And we end up in bed which certainly isn't a stretch. Then I fall in love with him all over again because let's face it—I still have feelings. Then after all that he tells me he's going back to Chicago. Another heartbreak. Only this time it will feel a hundred times worse. Do you still think this is a good idea?"

"This only ends in another stalemate if the two of you haven't learned anything from the last time."

Mika reached for her coffee cup and took a gulp, needing the fortification of caffeine.

"I'm not sure I follow you."

"I'm not talking about following me. I'm talking about following him. As in do it this time. Go with him."

Charlotte said it as if it was the most easy, natural thing in the world.

"My job–" Mika began but her friend shook her head.

"They have those in Chicago. Try again."

"Alex is settled–"

"They have schools in Chicago too, I'm told," Charlotte cut in. "Other kids he can make friends with."

"It's a big city. Lots of people," Mika replied quietly, already running out of arguments. She'd made them all before and they sounded just as hollow this time as they had years ago. "It doesn't matter because we're not in love and he hasn't asked me to go with him. It's moot."

But she could fall so easily…

"Cal wouldn't have kissed you unless he felt something. You feel it too. Are you really going to fight this?"

Was she? Her head and her heart were at war currently and both hurt from the skirmish.

"I have no idea what I'm going to do, honestly. I'm so confused I barely know which way is up. I thought I'd handled my feelings for Cal, to be honest. Placed him in his own little compartment and labeled it 'The Past'."

"Now he's your present," Charlotte replied crisply. "What do you plan to do about it? Run and hide or gather your courage and face it?"

Mika had to finally admit there wasn't any way to outrun her past. It had found her, kissed her, and made her feel things she hadn't in so long. It was bad and good and yes, kind of annoying all at the same time. She hadn't been consulted about whether she wanted this but here it was whether she liked it or not.

"I don't really have a choice. If I don't deal with Cal now he'll haunt me for the rest of my life."

"So what's the plan?"

"I have no idea. There is no plan except to survive the next few months but one thing is for certain. I'm done with trying to avoid him or make him feel guilty. From now on I deal with Cal straight on, no games. If he wants to spend time with Alex then that's fine and dandy with me."

"And if he wants to spend time with you?" Charlotte asked, a playful smile on her lips as she snagged another piece of bacon. "What will you do then?"

"You ask a lot of questions," Mika said instead of answering. She stood and went straight to the coffee pot, warming up her cup, studiously avoiding looking her friend in the eye.

"Michaela Adams, you don't fool me."

Mika had a terrible feeling she wasn't fooling anyone. Cal least of all.

Chapter Nine

'M ALL FINISHED up in the bedroom. That only leaves the table you want built for the back porch."

Cal was wiping his hands on a towel as he joined her in the dining room of the haunted house. Mika was at the table putting the finishing touches on some throw pillows for the parlor. She'd tried to keep her distance from Cal all week but he kept finding reasons to talk to her about this and that. Nothing of real importance but it still all seemed perfectly legitimate.

But it was still awkward as hell.

After the kiss they'd shared she simply didn't know how she was supposed to act. She'd had a week to think it over and she wasn't any closer to sorting out her emotions. All she knew was she still had feelings for Cal. Strong feelings that weren't going to fade away on their own. They hadn't after all this time so it looked like they were here to stay.

Now the only question was what was she prepared to do about it?

Mika was a woman who valued bravery and right now she wasn't a shining example. Her heart was crying out for one more chance with Cal and her head was in a semi-permanent state of muddle. It didn't make for the best combination.

"I can't believe how quickly you've worked through that list. I thought it would take twice as long."

Mika congratulated herself on how normal she sounded and not like the confused, sleep deprived woman she actually was at this moment. She handed him a bottle of water from the cooler at her feet, their fingers brushing just long enough to send a bolt of electricity straight up her arm and down to her already fluttering stomach.

"I like to keep busy. Dad doesn't have much work these days."

"Is he going to retire soon?"

Cal sat down in a folding chair with a soft groan. "I hope so, but he likes to stay busy so I guess a carpentry job every now and then isn't such a terrible thing. It's big jobs like this that I don't think he should be doing."

The haunted house was a huge job and Cal had donated every bit of his labor. It was above and beyond the call of duty, especially since he didn't call Applewood home any longer.

A small factoid she needed to remember.

"I don't know what we would have done without you."

She cursed silently as her voice sounded more breathless than she intended.

"You would have managed. You always have before." He tipped the bottle back and drained the last of the icy liquid. "Where's Alex tonight? I thought he was going to help me stain those chairs."

Mika plucked at a thread on her sweater. "He's, um, he's with Charlotte and her kids. He's spending the night. Then tomorrow night they'll stay at our house. We switch off so the boys can spend time together."

Cal's brows shot up and Mika's heart beat a little faster. Since they'd bared their souls they hadn't been alone – truly alone – but they were now. All the other volunteers had wandered off to their homes.

"I'm sure he and Kenny will have fun. So what do you have planned for your evening alone?"

Mika shrugged carelessly as if there wasn't a wall of living, breathing tension between them at the moment.

"Probably a hot bath and some pizza. Maybe read a good book."

Mika hadn't sat down long enough to read a book in years. She'd been too busy being mother and father to a little boy that needed both while making a living at the same time.

"How about dinner and a movie?"

It was her turn to look surprised. She had to consciously close her mouth as it was hanging open with shock.

Did he just ask her out on a date?

"I don't think that's a good idea, Cal."

"Why? Because we kissed the other night and you liked it? Well, I liked it too. I liked it so much I think we should do it again."

She wasn't prepared for this.

"I didn't like it."

That only made Cal grin and laugh because they both knew she was a big, fat liar. She'd loved that kiss and had been thinking about it constantly since it had happened.

"You're lucky lightning is busy elsewhere, sweetheart, or

you'd be fried. Now let's try this again. Would you like to go out tonight?"

"No," she mumbled, shoving papers willy-nilly into her bag and trying not to look him in the eyes. She needed to get the hell out of here because she was starting to feel weak. "I need to go home."

"No, you *want* to go home. You *need* to face the fact that there's still something between us. Don't you owe it to yourself to find out what it is?"

Mika slapped her purse down on the table, anger and frustration bubbling just underneath the surface as she held on to her temper by a thread. "You are such an arrogant ass. You think no woman can resist you."

Cal shook his head and stepped closer so she had to look up at him. "Not in the least. The fact is I'm not such a great bargain right now. A man in the midst of a mid-life crisis. Unemployed to boot. That's hardly irresistible. But I haven't stopped thinking about that kiss and I think you've done the same thing. I don't know where this might lead but I know that I want to follow where it goes. Tell me you don't feel the same."

"So what if I do? I know how this ends, Cal. I was there the last time, remember?"

"Not this time," Cal growled, wrapping an arm around her and yanking her close. Their bodies were melded together and she was swamped with his heady scent, her senses almost drunk. "I've thought a lot about us and there's nothing for me back in Chicago. I'm staying put this time."

With every fiber of her being she wanted to believe him. It would all be like a fairytale with her, Cal, and Alex living happily ever after in a home with a white picket fence.

She didn't believe in the Tooth Fairy anymore.

"You've rented the house for three months."

His smile widened and his arms tightened around her, their lips so close. "Sometimes I forget how news travels around here. It doesn't make any difference though. I've done a lot of thinking and I've decided to stay."

"You could never be happy here."

"The old me couldn't but I've changed, sweetheart. Already I feel less stressed and happier than I have in a long time. It's over with the FBI and I know it. I'll be lucky if they don't throw me out on my ass."

"So you'll take me as a consolation prize?"

The words came out more bitter than she'd planned but there was still too much anger in her heart to believe his sweet words.

"I'll take you as my second chance at happiness. I blew the first but I'm hoping you'll want to try again. What we have is rare and I realize that now. I think you know it too."

"When did you come to that conclusion?"

His large hand, callused and rough, cupped her cheek. "This morning, actually. I might be a little slow on the uptake but once I get there I'm all in. Now I'll ask again. Will you go out to dinner with me?"

"No."

"Say yes."

"No," she said again but it didn't have the force of the first one. He was looking at her with an expression of longing that she'd almost forgotten. "No."

"Coward," he whispered in her ear, his breath caressing her skin and sending sparks straight to her toes.

"Challenging me isn't going to work. And I'm not a coward."

"That's the damn truth. The woman I knew wouldn't have run from this, Mika. She wouldn't run away from her feelings. That's one of the things I loved about her. Her innate honesty. You were the first one to say I love you. You were courageous and I thought you were the most amazing woman I'd ever known. Hell, I still do."

How was she supposed to stay strong when all she wanted to do was collapse in his arms? It wasn't fair and it pissed her off but he was right about one thing. She'd changed since she became Alex's mother. She'd become a shadow of her former self, playing it safe at all times and eschewing risk. It hadn't happened overnight but here she was a real wimp. The kind of woman who could bore herself to tears.

"Fine. Just dinner."

"And a movie," he pressed but she shook her head in exasperation. He'd always been like this. Give the man an inch and he thought he was a ruler.

"Maybe a movie. Don't push me, Cal. I can easily just go home and eat in front of the television by myself."

"Okay, you win. Dinner and maybe a movie."

"What did you have in mind? The diner?"

Cal's arms loosened and he stepped back and began packing away his tools one by one. "Actually I heard about that new steak house in Virginia Beach and I've been wanting to try it. Are you game?"

He knew very well she loved a well-cooked filet with a baked potato on the side. Her answer was a given.

"Then I definitely need to change." She looked down at her faded blue jeans and white blouse, already second-guessing the entire evening. "Is that okay?"

"Of course. I can't go like this either. Why don't I pick you up in about an hour?"

Like a date. With kisses and stuff. She was such an idiot. Cal made her do things she wouldn't normally do.

"An hour," she echoed, grabbing up her things and making her way toward the car. She didn't want to think about how unwise the entire idea was. "I'll be ready."

As ready as she'd ever be.

Chapter Ten

CAL RAN HIS finger around his collar again as he and Mika sipped their coffee. They were sitting in the new steakhouse in Virginia Beach after enjoying a delicious meal and excellent service. The restaurant had certainly lived up to its hype and he and Mika had managed to keep the conversation light and friendly for most of the meal.

He was still nervous as hell. Everything he wanted was riding on this so the pressure was on. He'd always thrived on the adrenaline but the sweat pooling at the back of his neck was no joke. This tiny woman held his future happiness in her hands.

She was nervous too.

She fidgeted in her chair, crossing and uncrossing her legs while she jangled her foot to some beat that only she could hear. Now that dinner was drawing to an end she was playing with her spoon, her gaze riveted to the flatware as if it was the first utensil she'd ever seen in her life.

"So what do you think about a movie? I'll let you choose. They have them all here in Virginia Beach."

The Applewood cinema only showed two movies at a time and they were whatever Sam's wife enjoyed, which meant they were usually chick flicks of some sort where someone dies in the end and everyone cries. Not a car chase, alien, or superhero to be found.

"It's kind of late."

Mika still didn't look up, needlessly stirring her coffee, the china clinking with every turn of the spoon.

Cal quickly checked his watch and grinned. "It's nine o'clock. That's not late unless you're Alex's age. We're all grown up and we can stay out when it's not a school night."

Mika finally looked up at him a reluctant smile on her lips. "I'm usually passed out on the couch by nine-thirty. It's funny because I used to be such a night owl."

Laughing, he remembered a few crabby, cranky mornings but he'd always known the way to get on her good side. "I never could convince you that the sunrise was something worth getting up for. You once threw your alarm clock at me when we were going fishing."

"Why do fish get up so early anyway?" Mika wrinkled her nose and Cal had to quell the urge to kiss her right here at the table in front of all the other patrons.

"I doubt they have a big social life so they probably go to bed early."

Mika tapped her chin in thought. "I think they probably do. They swim around in schools so they're always socializing. I bet fish are all extroverts."

This was more like the woman he'd left behind. Zany. Challenging. Gorgeous.

When he'd picked her up tonight he'd had to put his tongue back in his head. Dressed in a little black dress that skimmed her thighs and showed just a hint of cleavage, she looked mouth-wateringly beautiful. She'd left her auburn hair down and all he could think about was running his fingers through those silky strands.

"I know what you're doing, sweetheart. You're trying to distract me from the original question. Do you want to go see a movie?"

"No," she sighed, setting her spoon down on the saucer with a clatter. "I want to go to the beach. I haven't been in ages. Will you take me?"

Moonlight, sand, and Mika frolicking on the shore. Hell yes, he'd take her. Then he'd kiss her under that moon and remind her of all the good things they'd had together.

✦ ✦ ✦

THE WATER WAS cold.

Mika danced in the soft sand as the waves lapped at her toes. Giggling as the foam tickled the soles of her feet, she reached out to grab Cal's arm and pull him in with her. They'd both taken off their shoes but mostly he'd stood there watching her act like a crazy loon.

It had been so damn long since she'd had…fun.

No worries in sight and nothing but the night ahead. Alex was safely with Charlotte. The haunted house was ahead of schedule. Even the term papers she'd assigned had been read and graded. There wasn't a speed bump in sight.

"Christ on a unicycle," Cal hissed as another wave crashed into their legs. "This water is like ice. Now I know why we only came here in the summer."

"It's not that bad," she protested, pulling him deeper until the water reached their knees. Well, her knees. He was much taller. "It's refreshing."

The full moon hung overhead and she could clearly make out his scandalized features. "If this is only refreshing you might like to take a dip into Lake Michigan in January. You'd love it."

Digging her toes into the sand, she closed her eyes and felt the in and out pull of the tide plus the gentle breeze on her face. She hadn't felt so alive in years and a huge part of it was this man.

She wanted to be the person she used to be.

She wanted to do that with Cal.

Mika opened her eyes and stepped closer to Cal before grabbing his shirt with both hands, the material bunched in between her fingers. She tugged on the fabric until they were almost nose to nose. This was the most important question of her life and she needed the answer. She couldn't wait to figure it out at some later date. It was now or never.

"Are you really staying in Applewood? Don't bullshit me, Cal. Tell me the truth. Are you staying?"

She'd practically shouted but thank the gods there wasn't anyone around. She couldn't drag her gaze away and they simply stood there for a long time looking into one another's eyes. She hoped he could see that she needed to know the truth and nothing but the truth.

"Yes," he finally said, his voice deep but still soft in the silence. "I'm staying. Applewood is home and so are you. I had a long talk with my mother on Sunday and she set me straight about a lot of things. I may not know what I'm going to do with the rest of my life but I know that I want you in it."

Mika wanted desperately to believe. Cal had evoked so many emotions in her since the day he'd walked back into her life. It was as if she'd been asleep for years but was now awakened, seeing everything clearly. So many mistakes, so many hurts. Was she arrogant to think they could wipe that away and start again?

"You're not sure about me, are you? I've never lied to you, Mika. In the past I never said that I'd stay. I never made you a promise I couldn't keep. So when I say to you now that I'm not going anywhere I'm telling the God's honest truth. Will you trust me?" Cal asked, his fingers tracing her jaw and taking her breath away. She'd been alone way too long and had missed his strong hands. "Maybe this will remind you that you can."

His lips were on hers and she gripped his shoulders as the world spun on its axis. The very breath seemed to be sucked from her body even as her heart sounded in her ears like a timpani. This was what she'd pushed out of her mind, told herself she didn't need.

Pleasure and warmth rushed through her veins as one of his hands slid up her ribcage to cup her breast. His thumb strummed the already hard nipple poking through the lace of her bra and the thin material of her dress. She pressed herself closer, wanting to feel every muscled inch of him against her own body. Right now he was everything and her world had narrowed to only the two of them on this deserted strip of beach.

His arm slid under her knees and she felt herself lifted out of the water and carried to the blanket he'd pulled from the back of his truck earlier. Dragging his lips away, he set her down gently before lying on top of her, his arms taking his weight and effectively caging her in.

She wouldn't have moved for the world.

The second kiss was completely different than the first. Cal took his time exploring every nook and cranny of her mouth as if they had eternity to just lie here under the stars and ignore the rest of the heartless, demanding world.

She slid her hands down his spine, feeling the muscles move and bunch under her palms. She pressed butterfly kisses to his jaw before blazing a trail down the cord of his neck, his pulse strong under her lips. His skin tasted slightly salty and she let her tongue lazily lap at the flesh until he groaned. His mouth and tongue glided down to her collarbone before beginning a sensual foray to the swell of her breast. His tongue snaked out and slid under the neckline of her dress and the lace of her bra, just skimming the edge of a pebbled bud.

Awash in sensation, she arched her back to give him more access as her hands continued their journey to catalog his every response to her touch, each moan and whisper amping her desire up that much higher.

She'd missed this and even if he left tomorrow she couldn't be sad that she'd experienced it.

One more time.

MIKA'S SKIN FELT like the finest satin and he greedily slid his hand under the skirt of her dress, up the warm flesh of her thigh. He brushed his fingers over her mound and then played with the lace elastic waistband of her panties, knowing she loved it when he teased her a little.

She moved restlessly underneath him and he chuckled at her impatience when she nipped at the cord of his neck, molding her soft curves to his hard body. It had simply been way too long since the last time he'd touched and held her this way. He must have been crazy to ever leave and he sure as hell wouldn't do it again. His career hadn't given him a fraction of the satisfaction ten minutes in her company had.

A white hot flame built in his abdomen as he kissed, licked, and nipped every inch of exposed flesh. Her lips tasted of wine and chocolate mousse and he couldn't get enough of her sweetness.

His fingertips sensuously glided over the spot where her hip met her thigh and she moaned as he tickled the skin before sliding up under the edge of her cotton panties. His thumb caressed the pearl between her legs while he eased one finger into her tight channel, already slick and hot. Her hips rolled as Cal found the sensitive spot deep inside that he knew so well and he slowly moved his finger in a circular motion while his thumb did the same on her swollen bud.

The catch of her breath and the trembling of her legs told Cal without any doubt that Mika was teetering on the edge. He added a second finger and Mika sobbed as her climax took over. Her tight walls clenched on his hand and he could feel the waves of her completion along with her panting breath. As Mika came down to earth she whispered his name in a soft voice that twisted his heart, hard and cruel. He'd never leave her again. Being with her like this was what had been missing from his life.

Scratch that. He hadn't had a life. He'd had an existence.

Cal held her, neither of them speaking for a long time until her hand wandered down his torso and rested on his hard length. Sucking in a tortured breath, he jerked away from her questing fingers and lifted them to his lips.

"Easy, sweetheart. Tonight is for you."

"But...you're...hard."

As solid steel and it fucking hurt, but he knew deep down that she wasn't ready for them to do more than this. She wasn't convinced of his sincerity. Right now this was her libido doing all the talking.

"I am but it won't kill me to wait. The cold, hard fact is you still don't believe me, do you? You think I still might leave. Until you can trust that what I say is the truth I don't think we should take this any further."

Mika slowly sat up and pulled her knees to her chest in a protective gesture. He'd guessed correctly. She wasn't there yet. She still couldn't believe in him and what was between them.

"I want to believe you," she finally said, her chin resting on her knees. "Nothing has been the same since you left."

"For me either and I plan to spend the next few weeks proving that to you. I want you to trust me again." He played with a strand of her silky hair, tickling her cute nose. "I need you to."

"How do you propose to do that?"

Mika reached out and captured his hand with hers, their fingers entwined. She looked wonderfully mussed, her hair tousled and her lips swollen from their kisses. The neckline of her dress was slightly askew and it made him want to press her back onto the grass and continue what they'd started.

But he didn't do it. Instead he chuckled and placed a kiss in the center of her palm before placing it on his heart where she could feel its heavy thud.

"I courted you once and won your love so I think I might be able to do it again. When was the last time a man made a fuss over you, Mika Adams? I'm going to bring you flowers, hold your hand, and steal kisses on your front porch swing. I'm going to let the whole town know that you're my girl. Will you let me do that? Will you let me earn your trust again?"

He held his breath as she gazed steadily into his eyes. Even in the dim light he could see the emotions flit across her features. First fear, then want, and finally hope.

"Yes, although I have to admit it's been a long time since I was courted. I may have forgotten how to act. You might need to take it easy on me in the beginning."

"Easy," he scoffed, a smile blooming on his face. "Baby, prepare to be wowed and wooed."

He had a mission and it was only the most important of his life.

No pressure.

Chapter Eleven

WOOED AND WOWED was an understatement.

Mika had been the recipient of flowers, candy, candlelight dinners, handheld strolls down Main Street, and even a stuffed bear that had been left on her front doorstep. She'd found him early one morning as she'd gone out to retrieve the newspaper. The furry brown teddy with big blue eyes had been holding her rolled up paper in its paws while being propped up on a sealed plastic container of pastries from the bakery.

She'd hugged that bear to her chest and felt tears prick the back of her eyes. He was truly trying to show her how he felt. Cal had always treated her well in the past but this time he'd taken it to a whole new level. She felt like a pampered princess.

"Mom, I'm hungry."

A plaintive wail cut through the serenity of the moment and Mika had to chuckle softly to herself.

So much for royalty. A mother's work was rarely glamorous and never finished. But it had been heaven for those few moments to bask in Cal's loving regard.

"Eggs and toast? Or just cereal?"

Alex had been particularly picky about his food lately, telling her certain things were "icky" when he ate them all the time. His usual staples of grilled cheese and chicken fingers were being replaced with more grown up fare. Mika wasn't against the transition in the least but it had come as something of a shock. Her baby was growing up so fast.

"Do you know how to make a cheese omelet?"

"Yes," she answered slowly, pouring him a glass of orange juice. "I do, but have you ever eaten one?"

"Cal had one for breakfast on Sunday when we met him at the diner. I want to try one. Can you do it?"

Cal. Of course.

Alex had a serious case of hero worship going. He trailed after Cal like a puppy, wanting to do everything the older man did right down to what he ate and how he dressed. Mika was happy that the two most important men in her life were getting along so well but there was a little part of her that felt a pang every time she saw them together. If Cal didn't keep his word he would break her son's heart. It was her job as Alex's mother to keep him safe from harm and here she was putting his love on the line.

It was one thing to do it to herself, but her son…

But with each passing day she believed in Cal a little more, the bricks surrounding her heart falling down one by one. He showed her in every way possible that she and Alex were the most important thing to him, even going as far as taking the little boy fishing early Saturday morning. Her son was blossoming under Cal's positive attention and Mika couldn't help but picture a future with the three of them as a family.

It was too soon to be thinking that way but she couldn't

seem to stop herself. Having Cal back in her life like this was bringing back all the reasons she'd fallen in love with him in the first place.

"Sure, I'll make you a cheese omelet. It's not difficult." Mika pulled herself from her reverie as her young son busied himself with putting his school books into his backpack. He was supposed to do it at night so they wouldn't rush around in the morning but more often than not she had to remind him. "Don't forget that permission slip for your field trip. I signed it and set it on your desk."

Quickly whipping up the omelet, Mika listened as her son regaled her with more tales of how amazing Cal was. Between the carpentry, the fishing, and the touch football in the front yard Alex was completely won over.

Mika still held out a small part of herself. The piece of her heart that was terrified of being hurt again. Cal had told her over and over that he wasn't going anywhere but it was scary to believe.

"Yoohoo!" Charlotte stuck her head around the front door as Kenny barreled into the house, book bag in hand. It was Mika's day to drop the boys at the elementary school. Charlotte would pick them up and take them to soccer practice. "Is that coffee I smell? I haven't had nearly enough."

Charlotte went straight to the cabinet and pulled down her favorite mug while Kenny and Alex disappeared into the living room to use the few brief minutes before school to play.

"Aren't those lovely flowers," Charlotte marveled with a wide smile, sniffing at the fragrant blooms in the glass vase. "Is this your second or third bouquet from Mr. Faulkner? Who knew he was such a romantic?"

"It's the third," Mika admitted but she was smiling as well. Cal had told her he was committed to making sure she had fresh flowers on her kitchen table at all times since he knew how much she loved them. "Cal's being…really great."

Charlotte rolled her eyes and laughed. "Is that code for I'm falling for him again because he's not only gorgeous, he's sweet and wonderful?"

"There's still a lot of questions unanswered. I'm not rushing into anything."

Charlotte downed half of her coffee in two gulps. "What's unanswered? Cal's hotter than a firecracker and I remember you saying he could kiss better than anyone else. He's also just a really good man. He never cheated on you. What's the issue? Is he simply too perfect?"

Cal wasn't perfect but she was beginning to believe they were perfect for each other and that was a dangerous proposition. It meant putting herself out there and that was something she hadn't done in a long time.

"I'm being cautious and if you were me you'd be the same. I have more than myself to think about."

"Alex adores Cal and Cal's good with kids. You're still young enough to have one or two of your own, you know."

Mika's fingers tightened on the slice of bacon and it crumbled back onto the plate. "What if he doesn't stay?"

"Then you go with him," Charlotte said softly, her smile disappearing. "Because having him in Chicago, or New York, or even Timbuktu is a hell of a lot more important than staying in Applewood because of some sort of loyalty to your job or Alex's school. Alex will make new friends and you can get a new job."

"You make it sound so easy."

Charlotte abandoned her coffee and stood in front of Mika, placing her hands on her shoulders and giving her a little shake. "You always want to talk about taking an idea to its logical conclusion, so let's do that. Let's say Cal wants to leave and you for some reason decide not to go along. So you stay here in Applewood and Alex grows older and goes away to college. Maybe he gets a job in another town and gets married. He can have a kid or two. Then his job transfers him to Los Angeles or Seattle. In the meantime you retire from teaching. So now Alex and your job are gone and you're sitting here in this house in this town with no man to love you. You're alone. I know some people might be okay with that but dammit, you deserve someone to love you, Mika. I'd hate to see you miss out on that."

Mika's throat clogged at the picture Charlotte had painted. "There are no guarantees."

"That's true. You could meet another man. Your relationship with Cal could fall apart even if you do follow him. But you've spent all this time trying to pretend that you didn't make a decision when Cal left. *Inaction* is a decision, Mika. You decided to let Cal leave and if he goes and you stay you'll have decided to do it a second time. Make no mistake, just sitting here and waiting for him to come back is a decision."

"He says he's staying."

Charlotte rinsed her cup in the sink before reaching for her purse. "Then believe him. Show some trust in a man that has never lied to you and has only wanted your happiness. We should all be so lucky."

Everything was beginning to become clear. Cal was doing all he could to build some sort of future for them. What was she doing?

Doubting. Impeding. Complaining because every little thing didn't go her way.

It was time to show Cal how she felt.

Chapter Twelve

"T HERE'S MORE EGGROLLS if you're still hungry."

Cal pushed the white paper box closer to Mika but she groaned and patted her stomach. They were enjoying an early dinner and a movie before she had to pick up Alex from Charlotte's house. It was Kenny's birthday and Charlotte had taken her son plus a few of his friends into Virginia Beach for a bowling party.

"I couldn't eat another bite but it was delicious. Alex only ever wants to order a pizza."

Cal chuckled and began to clean up the food, stowing the leftovers in his refrigerator. "It's nice that there are more places to order from than there used to be. When I lived here before it was pizza or nothing. And they closed at ten in the evening."

"We've moved up in the world," Mika teased with a smile. "We have two places for pizza, Chinese takeout, and even a fast food burger joint. It's like we're in the twentieth century."

"You mean twenty-first," Cal corrected but she shook her head.

"No, I meant the twentieth but I'm sure we'll get to the next century eventually. We're not in any hurry. We locals are funny like that."

Applewood certainly did march to its own drummer. The people enjoyed the small town atmosphere that was steeped in traditions from another decade.

But it still had Wi-Fi.

Cal popped the movie she'd picked out into the player and they settled on the couch, her head on his shoulder and her thigh pressed against his. Since he'd called a halt to their lovemaking that night on the beach he'd worked hard to court her and win her trust. It hadn't been easy to tame his more base instincts but Mika was worth it. He needed her to know this wasn't a game.

About ten minutes into the film he knew he'd been had.

"What are we watching?"

A beat of silence and then a giggle.

"Um, a romantic comedy about two friends who fall in love."

Cal groaned and twisted around so he could see her delighted expression.

"You promised."

They had watched three chick flicks in a row – that she'd chosen – and she'd promised to choose something else for tonight.

"I know and I feel badly about that, but this one just came out and all the teachers were talking about it at school today."

Mika held up the DVD cover with an embracing couple on the front. Her lower lip stuck out in a pout and her eyes twinkled with merriment. She'd learned that from Alex or perhaps he'd learned it from her. Either way Cal wasn't falling for it a fourth time.

"You promised," he repeated. "It didn't have to be a bloody war movie but come on, sweetheart. At the rate we're watching these my testosterone is going to drain away and I'll find myself crying on the couch craving chocolate."

Mika slapped her hand over her mouth to try and contain the peals of laughter but it didn't quite come off. He watched as her mirth turned to pure glee, tears leaking from her eyes and sliding down her cheeks.

"I can just see it too. My big strong alpha male sitting on the couch with a pint of ice cream watching *Bridget Jones' Diary*. That is too funny."

She was finding this far more amusing than he did but he loved watching her truly let go of her inhibitions and relish life in this way. In the past few weeks she had a glow…a zest…that was simply mesmerizing.

He loved her. Again.

Maybe he always had and he'd simply tucked it away for a while.

This was the woman he wanted to spend eternity with. He could only hope she felt the same.

That she felt *something* for him. As long as she still had feelings there was hope.

It felt like a vise was wrapped around his chest as he stared down at her flushed face and shiny, parted lips. She was so goddamn beautiful and he was one lucky son of a bitch.

Hopefully.

"I'm *your* alpha male, huh? Very possessive, honey."

He leaned over and tickled her ribs with his fingers, sending her into more gales of laughter, her face turning bright red.

"Don't do that. You know I'm ticklish."

Mika slapped ineffectually – and half-heartedly – at his hands as she writhed on the couch, the sound of her giggles more wonderful than any love song or symphony. Eventually she slipped off the cushions and he followed her to the floor, his weight pressing her into the rug.

He dragged his lips across hers again and again until their breath was ragged and Mika's fingers were dug into his shoulders. Kissing a trail down her body, he paused at the sensitive spot where neck met shoulder and gave the creamy skin a nip before soothing it with his tongue.

His hands rested on her hips and he itched to explore farther, stripping away every stitch of clothing so he could kiss her everywhere. She was especially fond of a tongue teasing her belly button, but instead of pulling the shirt over her head he took a deep breath to get his arousal under control.

"What's wrong?" Mika pushed at his chest and he sat back on his haunches. "You kind of stopped."

It hadn't been easy either. He was hot and hard, ready to take her but he had to hold back no matter how much he wanted to give in. He'd meant it when he said they wouldn't make love until she truly believed in him.

"I was thinking we should just slow this all down. Maybe I should take you home."

Mika sat up and reached for the hem of his t-shirt, sliding her fingers underneath. His flesh burned everywhere she touched. "No. You can't do this again. It was sweet that you wanted us to wait but I think we've gone past that. I want to be with you and I know you want to be with me."

She looked pointedly at the large bulge in his pants.

"If you can't believe that I'm—"

He never finished the sentence. Her kiss cut him off and their tongues tangled together in a sensual dance. When she finally pulled back she was wearing a smile, her brown eyes like soft velvet.

"I believe you."

Three simple words but they held so much meaning.

The barrier he'd built around his heart tumbled down and love suffused each and every cell. The future he didn't even dare dream about was within his grasp.

✦　✦　✦

"I BELIEVE YOU," Mika said again softly. "I know you're telling me the truth."

Skimming his ribcage with her palms, she tugged his t-shirt up and over his head, baring his muscular torso to her hungry gaze. Wide shoulders and flat abs, his chest had the perfect smattering of dark, silky chest hair and she ran her fingers through it before raining kisses over every inch of exposed flesh she could reach.

She was pulling at his zipper as she pressed her lips to a flat, male nipple. Her tongue darted out to give it a lick before turning her attention to its twin. Cal groaned and buried his fingers in her hair as she skimmed her mouth south, capturing the tab of the zipper between her teeth and lowering it slowly.

"Christ, Mika. You make me crazy," Cal growled. "Slow down."

Going slower was not an option.

The urgency she'd felt in his arms each night since he'd come back was almost overwhelming now. Her heartbeat pounded in her ears and her hands shook as she caressed his tanned skin. The scent of his skin teased her nostrils and she skimmed her fingertips over the denim covered ridge in his jeans. His thigh muscles tensed but his jaw remained determined.

"I don't want to slow down. I've been waiting too long."

It had been an eternity since they were this close and she didn't want to wait a minute longer.

"You're going to be the death of me, woman. I'm trying to be romantic and tender."

"And I love you for it. But we can be romantic next time when I'm not feeling so needy. You know how I like it, Cal."

He ought to. He was the one that had turned her into something of a sex maniac, for him only, of course. He'd encouraged her to experiment and try new things and she'd figured out early in their relationship she loved being taken hard, fast, and with no mercy. It was exactly what she needed for her desperate mood.

His hands rubbed up and down her thighs in a soothing motion but it only served to enflame her desire and send a white hot heat streaming to her toes. "I remember, sweetheart. I know what you need."

His voice was low, a sweet caress to her overheated senses and she surrendered to him as he quickly stripped her clothes from her body, heat streaking to her slit from every touch of his rough fingers.

Shoving his pants and boxers down his legs, he kicked them aside onto the forgotten mound of clothes on the floor. They'd be creased and wrinkled later but Mika couldn't summon the will to care, her eyes only for this one man.

Cal bent his head and sucked a hard nipple into his mouth, his teeth worrying the sides until her fingers dug into his scalp and she cried out with the sensations that seemed to go directly to her swollen clit. With a chuckle he turned his attention to the other taut peak, lapping at it before blazing a wet trail with his mouth down her quivering abdomen.

Pressing kisses to her inner thigh, he swirled his tongue around her swollen bud and then teasingly traced her inner folds, making the room tilt and spin with every single touch. Her fingers curled into his short, dark hair and her thighs pressed against his head as her arousal took her closer and closer to the edge. Expertly he kept her dancing there, never sending her over but driving her almost delirious with his skilled hands and mouth.

Her flesh was slick with sweat and her back arched with pleasure as Cal pressed first one, then two fingers into her slick channel. Her hips bucked and he placed his large hand on her lower belly, his thumb sweeping back and forth over her clit.

"Come apart for me, sweetheart. I want to watch you." Cal's voice was low and cajoling yet infinitely sensual as he leaned down and whispered in her ear. His breath tickled her neck and she shivered in helpless response. "Do it for me."

Her orgasm slammed into her hard and lights sparkled behind her lids. She rode his fingers until the very end, his name on her lips.

"Cal."

"That was so damn beautiful, sweetheart. I don't know how

I lived without you but I don't intend to find out." His hand caressed her jaw, sweeping her hair back from her damp face. "Open your eyes. I want you to know it's me."

Her lids fluttered and Mika could see Cal above her looking down with so much love it made her heart ache. How could she have turned away from him in the beginning? The two of them were made for each other. All the intervening years had simply been leading up to this. Tonight.

Positioning himself in between her thighs he entered her slowly, taking care not to hurt her. It had been a long time and Cal wasn't a small man. She was wet and ready for him and he was able to slide in to the hilt without causing any pain, her walls stretching to accommodate his generous size.

Mika anchored her fingers on his muscled backside and she wrapped her legs around his waist.

"Now, Cal. Do it now."

The words came out far more desperate than she'd planned but Cal didn't seem to care. He began to move slowly at first and then faster as she whispered urgently in his ear all the things she wanted them to do. She had a laundry list of dirty, naughty things she'd fantasized about when he'd been gone and she was determined to check them off one by one in the not too distant future. Sex with Cal had always been good. Adventurous too.

Cal rode her hard and fast, just the way she liked it, her arousal building until she was near the peak once again. Her fingernails dug into his buttocks as he reached between them and pressed his thumb on her swollen clit.

Mika screamed his name as her climax exploded, her toes curling with the wash of pleasure that ran straight through her over and over until she was wrung out and sated.

Cal found his own completion and she watched mesmerized when he threw his head back, his jaw tight and his teeth snapped together. He stiffened and then groaned before slumping on top of her, pressing kisses to her damp skin and making her giggle.

Mika was happy. And sexually satisfied too.

She couldn't remember the last time she'd felt this euphoric but she was sure it was with this man. His presence made everything right.

"I know I'm crushing you and I swear I'm going to move. Any minute now. Just as soon as I start breathing again."

Mika let her palms skim down his spine, his skin warm to the touch. "You're fine. It feels good."

Cal heaved himself off and rolled onto his back, taking her with him and tucking her into his side. "You won't be saying that when you run out of oxygen."

"I won't be saying anything if I run out of oxygen."

Laughter bubbled up and she luxuriated in the sheer joy of being this close to him. This was love and she'd almost missed out due to sheer fear and stubbornness.

Cal reached for his pants and snagged his phone from his pocket to check the time. "We have a little while before we have to pick up Alex. We could take him for an ice cream sundae if you're in the mood."

Cal was always thinking about not only her but Alex too. Another reason she'd fallen for him again. He'd matured while he was away and become a man she could depend on no matter what might happen.

"I think that's a great idea but I want to say something first."

She propped herself up on her elbow and gazed into his eyes. They didn't really need to say it. One look at either of them told the story but she was tired of being the scared female she'd become. She wanted to be brave and fierce. She wanted to set a good example for her son about reaching out and grabbing life and love. "I want to say that I love you. Very much. Thank you for not giving up on me."

Cal's Adam's apple bobbed as he swallowed hard. "I love you too. I'd never give up. We've been around and around and here we are. I think we're meant to be together. I swear to you here and now that I'm going to get my shit together and become the kind of man you deserve to spend your life with. The kind of man you'd trust to guide Alex. I'm sort of drifting right now but I won't be for long. I promise you."

She believed him. Cal had been good at everything he'd ever tried so he could certainly find a new vocation. One that made him happy and fulfilled.

"I didn't mean for this to get all mushy." Mika wrinkled her nose and giggled. "I know you hate that."

"I think I can make an exception for you. Now we have about forty-five minutes. Where were we?"

"Naked and happy," she sighed, laying back down on the rug and beckoning to him. "We have just enough time."

Together at last, they had all the time in the world.

Chapter Thirteen

"**M**IKA. ALEX. THIS is my friend Jon Rudnick from over in Virginia Beach."

Cal was happy his friend had been able to join them for opening night at the haunted house. It was the perfect autumn evening, crisp but not too cold, with the crunch of leaves underneath their feet.

"Nice to meet you."

Mika smiled and shook Jon's hand and so did Alex before she motioned to the refreshment table groaning under the weight of delectable food. On the first night of the Autumn Festival everyone went all out and provided a dish for the buffet. There would be dinner, a few speeches, and then the food would be whisked away and the house would be open for business. It had been this way since before Cal was born and it would probably be the same for Alex's children.

"Wow, this is some spread," Jon enthused as they all filled their plates. "I may have to make two trips. Everything looks so good."

"I usually make at least two if not three," Cal agreed, piling a scoop of pistachio salad next to some baked beans. "You won't go hungry here, that's for sure. Alex, make sure you try some of my mother's famous chocolate pie. It's legendary."

Cal had helped his mother make those pies. She'd sat and directed and he'd done the grunt work. They'd turned out pretty damn good if he did say so himself.

The four of them found an unoccupied folding table outside close enough to the bonfire to feel its warmth without the messy smoke flying in their faces. When Alex excitedly asked Jon what it was like to be a real-life former Navy SEAL the conversation naturally turned to Cal and his friend's time in the military.

Cal's phone lit up and he dug it out of his front shirt pocket, frowning at the screen. "Excuse me, I need to take this."

Stepping away, he swiped the screen and pressed the cell to his ear, listening in disbelief. The call was from his former boss at the FBI and the investigation into Cal's actions during the Alan Morton case was complete. He listened numbly to the words, not really comprehending what was being said. When they were done talking Cal hit the end button and shoved the phone back into his pocket, rejoining Jon, Mika, and Alex.

He must have had a strange expression because Mika placed her hand over his. "Is everything okay?"

"The FBI's investigation on me is done."

Sympathy in her gaze, she squeezed his fingers. "I'm so sorry. It's just not fair."

"You got a raw deal, bro. They're losing a good man," Jon agreed, nodding his head.

"No. It's not that." Cal was still so stunned he was having a hard time expressing what he'd heard. "I was cleared. Of every-thing. Trainor asked me when I could be back in Chicago. They have a new undercover assignment for me."

Even in his deepest heart of hearts Cal had never expected the investigation to go his way. He'd been sure it was all a sham and he would be politely asked to resign, best case scenario. But here he was with a second chance at his chosen career. He was a damn good agent and he knew it. He'd put countless criminals behind bars in his years and the job was still challenging…

He didn't want to go back.

Cal was home. Applewood and small town life had grown on him these last two months. Add in the love of his life and he couldn't imagine why he would ever want to leave.

Silence stretched awkwardly and Jon patted Alex on the shoulder, pointing to the buffet.

"What do you say we go and find some more dessert? I think I see a dark chocolate cake over there and some vanilla pudding."

The two of them loped back into the warehouse leaving Cal and Mika alone at the table. Before he could tell her he wasn't about to leave she pressed two fingers to his lips.

"You don't have to say anything. I know you didn't think you would be cleared but now you have another chance."

She didn't understand at all.

"Sweetheart, let me explain–"

"No," Mika shook her head, her tone urgent. "You don't have to explain. Things have changed."

Cal finally snapped out of his reverie and grabbed at both of her hands. "I told you I wasn't going anywhere and I meant it, Mika. I'm staying here."

Tears shone in her eyes and she gave him a tremulous smile. "I don't want you to stay because of a promise you made to me. I want you to be happy and I don't want to stand in your way."

Cal had changed in more ways than one.

"Your belief in me means more than I can ever tell you." A lump in his throat made it hard to speak. "I love you, Mika, and I want to make a life here with you. You, me, and Alex. I think Applewood is a better place for him to grow up too. Wherever you are is home and that's good enough for me."

"I just want—"

"Are you trying to get rid of me?" Cal teased with a raised brow. "I tell you I love you and I want to stay and you try and talk me out of it. I might get a complex here."

Her brilliant smile was all he needed to make everything okay. The man that needed to climb the ladder and receive his validation from people he barely gave two shits about had finally grown the hell up. There were few people in the world whose opinion mattered to him and one of them was sitting right here.

"I'm glad you're staying. I've got big plans for next year's haunted house."

Cal laughed and leaned over to brush his lips against hers. "I can't wait to hear all about it, sweetheart. Consider me your willing slave."

"Does this mean you're going to join your father's carpentry business? I'm sure Abe would love that."

He'd thought long and hard about this very subject. Mika wasn't getting much of a bargain in this relationship. Cal was middle-aged and unemployed, not a great combination. She could do a hell of a lot better than him and so finding a new career was high on his list of things to do.

"No, I don't see myself doing that. The fact is," he admitted sheepishly, "I'm not sure what I want to be when I grow up."

"Something will come along when you least expect. I believe in you."

Mika couldn't possibly know how amazing those four words made him feel.

✦   ✦   ✦

MICHAELA COUNTED THE cash box with a smile of satisfaction. It had been a good opening night and the evening wasn't over yet. The haunted house wouldn't close for another hour.

"Marion, go ahead and lock up these receipts in the safe. I'll make a bank run in the morning."

"Will do. Where's Cal and Alex? And that gorgeous man that came with you tonight? Is he single?"

Marion was happily married so Mika knew the questions were only in fun. "That man is Jon Rudnick. He was in the Navy with Cal and no, he is not single. He has a girlfriend named Alison and he's talked about her all night. As for Cal and Alex…Cal's with Jon and Alex is with Kenny playing glow in the dark soccer with the other kids."

Marion frowned and shook her head. "Charlotte came in here about thirty minutes ago to say goodnight. She had all three kids in tow. Alex can't be with Kenny."

"Maybe they haven't actually left yet." Mika handed the bag with the cash back to Marion. "I'll just take a walk over to the field."

The makeshift soccer field was next door to the warehouse and it only took a minute for Mika to walk there. There were plenty of lights from the warehouse and the adjoining parking lot illuminating the grassy area but the running and shouting boys were almost a blur. When they stopped for a moment she was able to scan for Alex and her heart stopped for a moment when she didn't see him playing with the other boys.

"Jake!" Mika called, motioning to one of her son's classmates. "Have you seen Alex?"

The little boy screwed up his face and shrugged. "He left a while ago. I don't know where he was going."

Another skipped beat of her heart but she pushed down the fear that was beginning to build. No mother liked her son to be out of her sight for long and she was no exception. "Thank you. If you see him tell him to come back to the haunted house."

Jake scampered off and Mika turned back around and headed to the warehouse. Ten minutes later she'd scoured every inch of the property including the parking lot but to no avail. Pulling her cell from her pocket she dialed Charlotte's number praying Alex had somehow gone home with them.

"Mika, I didn't expect to hear from you. Is everything okay there?"

Settling into a chair in the ticket office, Mika nervously twisted a strand of hair around her finger. "I'm not sure. Is Alex with you?"

"No, when I picked up Kenny from the soccer field Alex said he was going to find you. I watched him head that way. Mika, what's going on? Is Alex missing?"

Her fingers tightened on the phone as emotion strangled her ability to speak. "I can't find him anywhere. I'm sure he's around here but…"

Her words trailed away as she swallowed a painful sob. Charlotte was speaking to her husband in the background for a moment before she came back on the phone.

"I'm coming back there to help you look," she stated. "You're right, I'm sure he's just playing somewhere but two will find him faster than one. Give me five minutes to get there."

The line went dead and Mika stared at the phone trying to keep herself calm. Perhaps Alex had wandered off with one of his friends from school. She should go talk to all the other parents.

"Sweetheart, are you okay?"

Mika looked up to see Cal, his brows pulled down in concern. Licking her dry lips, she gave herself a mental shake. She wasn't doing anyone any good in this state.

"I can't find Alex. He's not playing soccer. He isn't with Charlotte and Kenny. And I looked all over. This isn't like him."

Lately Alex had been chafing at the restrictions but he knew the rules about being out after dark and they didn't include the freedom to run around without his mother's permission.

Mika might not be Alex's biological mother but she had a mother's instinct. Something wasn't right.

Cal pulled his phone from his pocket. "I'll call Sheriff Dan and then we'll get organized and look for him. He can't have gone too far."

Alex could be alone and frightened somewhere. He didn't like the dark all that much and still wanted a night light in his room. Mika needed to get to him as quickly as possible.

"I'll look in the parking lot again and talk to the other mothers," she said but Cal caught her arm keeping her from leaving the office.

"We need to organize a grid search, Mika. That way we

know that no square foot has been overlooked. Just give me ten minutes and we'll do this."

She jerked her elbow away, anger rising in her chest and mixing with the fear already residing there. "Something could happen to him in ten minutes. I need to get to my baby, Cal. He might be hurt or alone."

"That's the exact reason we need to do this by the book." Their gazes collided and Cal placed his hands on her shoulders, leaning forward so only she could hear his words. "I'm begging you to trust me, sweetheart. This is something I know, something I've been trained for. Let me help you."

Her stomach was twisted into knots of growing terror but she swallowed hard and nodded, not trusting her own voice. This was his job, or at least it had been. If anyone could find a missing little boy it was Cal.

"I'm just scared. He's my baby."

"We're going to get your baby back but you have to trust me, okay?"

Mika nodded and then Jon stepped forward, the affable man she'd met earlier wiped away and in its place an intense, focused military man. "I want to help. I can start gathering volunteers to search and getting them organized."

"Do that. We'll line everyone up shoulder to shoulder and send each group in four different directions."

Shaking with fright, Mika allowed the man she loved to do the very thing he excelled at. She'd trust him with her own life and with Alex's too.

It was the longest, most excruciating ten minutes of her life.

Chapter Fourteen

❧

S HERIFF DAN TOOK notes of what Alex was wearing and the last place he was seen. Charlotte had indeed showed up and Cal had put her in charge of keeping Mika somewhat calm. Right now the woman he loved was positively terrified and all he wanted to do was pull her into his arms and tell her everything was going to be fine. However, he didn't have that luxury at this particular moment.

Thankfully years of training had kicked in and Cal felt confident they would find Alex nearby cold, scared, and alone but safe and sound.

"I've done a preliminary inventory and so far no children here at the festival are unaccounted for," Jon stepped back into the office, his demeanor all business. Cal was reassured that his friend was helping. He needed someone he trusted so he could bounce ideas around. "The volunteers are also ready. The local hardware store is sending over their entire stock of flashlights so we should be well equipped."

With a grim smile Sheriff Dan shoved the pad back into his jacket pocket. "I'm going to defer to you two young men on this since you have more missing person training than I do. Just tell me what you need from me and I'll make it happen."

Sheriff Dan had been the head lawman in this town for as long as Cal could remember. In fact, when he'd moved back he'd been shocked to see Dan still wearing a badge. He had to be seventy if he was a day.

"I'd like your deputies to run the grid search while Jon and I search those woods over there."

Dan nodded but stopped in front of Mika on the way out. "Now don't you worry about this, Micheala. We're going to find your boy. Your man knows what he's doing and this ain't the first lost child I've located in all my years here in Applewood. They're usually fast asleep under a tree somewhere having lost all track of time."

Cal liked hearing that he was Mika's man. It felt good to belong to someone even if it was under shitty circumstances like these. But then Cal had no intention of not finding Alex safe and unharmed.

"I know. Thank you, Sheriff." Mika gave him a watery smile and sniffled, a wadded up tissue pressed to her red nose. "I know we'll find him."

The sheriff strode out of the office and back to the deputies and volunteers while Cal checked his cell again to ensure he had plenty of battery power.

Ten minutes were up and it was time to get going.

"Mika, I want you to stay here in case Alex comes back. Jon and I are going to search those woods on the other side of the soccer field."

Her back ramrod straight, Mika pressed her lips together, her fists clenched at her sides.

"Fuck you, Cal. I'm not waiting around while my son is missing. It's been ten minutes and now I'm done sitting here with my thumb up my ass. I'm going to look for Alex."

Cal's mouth dropped open at Mika's salty language. She rarely dropped the f-bomb but it only showed him that she was scared to death and needed a physical outlet for that fear. He could give her that although that hadn't been his original plan.

"Fine. Charlotte, can you stay here? If Alex shows up you can call Mika's phone. Mika, is your phone fully charged?"

His abrupt change of attitude must have shocked her. She stood there for a moment, her forehead wrinkled and her head tilted to the side in confusion, but then she seemed to grasp that he'd given in and she nodded, holding out her cell for his inspection.

After a cursory glance he grabbed two flashlights, handing one to Jon. "Then let's go. It's already completely dark and the temperature is beginning to drop."

Alex had been wearing a jacket but the wind was starting to pick up.

The three of them hiked across the field and into the small wood right next to it. Cal easily found the trail and they took turns calling to Alex as loudly as possible, then listening for any reply he might make.

Mika was holding up well although her expression was stoic. She didn't say much as they walked but he could tell she was barely holding herself together. The realization slammed into him that at one point in his life he'd expected this woman to leave Alex with her parents and come to him in Chicago. There was no way she could ever have done that. When they'd placed that baby in Mika's arms he'd been hers from that moment since her sister wasn't capable of caring for him.

Her staying hadn't been because she didn't love Cal enough. She'd simply loved Alex too much. And damn if that didn't make her even more lovable.

They came to a fork in the trail and stopped, their ears perked for any tell-tale noise.

"Jon, this is where we're going to separate. If you follow that trail it will take you to the right corner of this wood."

Jon had GPS on his phone and he noted their current location with a nod of his head.

"I'll call you if I find anything." Jon reached out and squeezed Cal's shoulder. "Don't worry, we'll find him."

"Thanks for being here and helping."

"You guys throw a hell of a festival."

Mika placed her hand on Jon's arm. "Thank you so much. I mean it."

"Any time, and I mean that too," Jon replied before quietly heading down the right fork.

Cal and Mika took the left, alternating calls with silence, their voices growing hoarse from the yelling and the cold. He could see that Mika's demeanor had grown bleak as time passed although he'd checked his cell phone and they hadn't been out even forty-five minutes yet.

"How are we going to find him if he's in here? I can hardly see a thing."

Cal grasped her icy hand in his and rubbed the fingers to warm them. "When I was Alex's age I used to play in this wood almost every day in the summer and after school when the weather was good. I know it like the back of my own hand and I doubt it has changed that much except that the trees are thicker and taller."

More had changed but he didn't want Mika to worry. Enough was the same that there was no danger of them getting lost. They could concentrate on the more important task of finding Alex.

"Alex!" Mika called, her voice sounding loud in the night quiet. "Alex!"

It was then that Cal heard a distinct whine and he stopped, immediately holding up his hand when Mika would have called to her son again. He waited for what seemed like an eternity and then heard the whine again right before a distinct bark.

A dog. Hopefully Alex and a dog.

"Alex!" Cal bellowed louder than before, his throat almost raw. "Alex!"

The sound was faint but Cal heard it. Apparently Mika did as well because she grabbed his arm and started charging down the path. Cal had to rein her in, slowing her down so he could listen.

"Easy, babe. Don't run off on me," Cal warned, keeping his voice low. "We stay together."

"He's there! I know that's my baby." He could hear the tears in her voice and tried to keep her steady. This was the break he'd been hoping for since the little boy had gone missing.

"Keep calling to us, Alex! Keep yelling so we can find you!"

"We need to follow his voice," Cal whispered urgently. "Focus in on that. We're close, I can feel it."

It was hard to believe he could hear anything over the blood rushing in his ears like a tidal wave but another faint call came from just ahead along with several loud barks.

With a bead on where the sounds were coming from Cal sped up with Mika right by his side. There was a clearing just ahead and his gut was telling him that was exactly where Alex was located. They didn't need to call to Alex anymore as the dog was now howling its head off and making Cal's job almost too easy. When he broke through the brush and into the clearing, he almost screamed with relief when he saw Alex sitting on the ground next to a tree with his arms around a small, dirty puppy.

"Alex!" Mika bolted ahead and snatched her son up into her arms, rocking him as tears coursed down her face. The puppy whined indignantly at being ignored but promptly sat down as if waiting for his turn to be cuddled. "Alex, we've been looking for you everywhere! You know you're not supposed to be out after dark by yourself!"

Alex allowed the bone-crushing hug for a short time but then began wriggling to be free.

"Mom! You're squishing me."

Mika loosened her hold but didn't let go, instead leaning back so she could run her gaze from tennis shoes to the cowlick in Alex's short brown hair, assessing for any injury small or large. Other than a few tearstains and a lot of dirt, the boy appeared to be unharmed.

"Are you okay? Are you hurt?" Her hands ran down Alex's arms and legs urgently and Cal was mesmerized by the mother's love glowing on her face. He'd been such an idiot to leave and miss this, the nurturing yet fiercely protective side of her. She'd been like a momma bear tonight protecting her cub and it was unbearably beautiful to behold.

Alex denied being hurt and Cal knelt down to check for himself, his own throat tightening up at the thought of anything happening to the young man. Cal had loved Mika for years but Alex had wormed his way into Cal's heart in a matter of weeks.

"You okay, buddy?" Cal pulled out his cell phone and sent a text to Jon and also the sheriff so they could call off the search. "We were worried about you. How did you end up here?"

"I was heading to find you, Mom, but then I saw Henry and we played for awhile. I followed him here but then it got dark and I couldn't find my way back. So I sat down and waited for you to find me. I knew you would."

Mika slapped her forehead and groaned but Cal simply smiled and helped the boy to his feet. "Henry, huh? Did you give him that name or does he belong to someone?"

"I gave him that name. I found him playing in the bushes by the soccer field. I think he likes me. Can we keep him, Mom? Please? Please?"

The boy certainly knew when to pick his moments. Mika was so damn relieved and grateful to find Alex safe and sound she might just actually let him keep the puppy.

Mika still had one arm around Alex but she rubbed the back of her neck with the other hand, a sigh escaping her lips. "He might have a family that loves him."

Alex shook his head vigorously. "He doesn't! He doesn't have a collar or anything and he's real lonely. Please, Mom. I'll take good care of him. I'll walk him and feed him. I promise."

Cal had to muffle his chuckle at Alex's earnest plea. Cal had made the very same one when he was about the boy's age and it had been for another stray canine that had wandered into the yard. Of course he'd fallen down on that promise and his mother had often done the feeding and the walking but Cal had loved that dog for fifteen years before he'd had to let him go to the Rainbow Bridge. He hoped Mika would give in but he wouldn't interfere. If she didn't allow Alex to have the dog Cal would take the pup in himself. He loved animals but had always worked too many hours to have one.

"I can't believe I'm saying this but if he doesn't have another family then I guess he can stay." The boy's face split into a grin and he jumped into the air with a shriek of unbridled joy. "But you will help take care of him, Alex."

"I will, Mom. Can he sleep on my bed?"

Mika closed her eyes in abject surrender before opening them again and nodding. "After he has a bath. You and he both. You're filthy and he smells."

Cal scooped up the wriggling puppy in his arms and received a few wet, doggy kisses for his trouble. "How about we get back to the warehouse and out of the cold. I bet this dog could use some dinner."

"I'm hungry, too," Alex piped up clearly untroubled and un-scathed by his adventure after dark. Cal and Mika, on the other hand, surely had sprouted more gray hairs and lost a few years off their life.

"Of course you are. Hiking in the woods makes everyone hungry," Mika agreed, her features starting to relax for the first time in over an hour, although Cal was sure she would break down later when it was safe. Once Alex was tucked safely into bed she was going to need someone to hold her and chase the nightmares of what might have been away.

By the time they reached the fork in the trail Jon was there waiting for them, a grin on his face. He took the squirmy puppy so that Cal could lift an exhausted Alex up for a piggyback ride. They hiked as quickly as possible back to the haunted house where the sheriff and a crowd of people were there to greet them.

Sheriff Dan stepped forward, a big smile on his face, and congratulated them on a job well done. Alex and Henry were wrapped in blankets and fed, Mika never far from her child, fussing over him and kissing his forehead every now and then.

Jon slapped Cal on the back. "I think I'll get on the road now. It looks like all's well that ends well. I wish it would always be that way."

"Listen, thanks for everything. It was great having you here."

"I didn't really do anything." Jon shrugged and laughed. "It was kind of nice not having anyone shoot at me though. But I don't think I want to get too used to that."

"It meant everything that you were here tonight for the festival and then helped us look for Alex. Really, man, thanks."

Jon looked embarrassed so Cal didn't push it anymore. A damn good friend, Jon never asked for recognition or thanks and that made him a rare breed. He bid everyone goodbye and got behind the wheel of his massive truck, waving as he pulled out of the parking lot.

Cal wrapped his arms around Mika and pulled her close. She slumped into his embrace, worn out from the emotional toll the events had taken. He hoped she could sleep tonight.

"How about we go home? We'll clean them up and then get you in a nice hot bath with a glass of wine."

"That sounds like heaven." Mika pressed her cheek to his chest and once again he thought his heart would split in two pieces, not able to hold the tsunami of love that enveloped him. She was everything he'd ever wanted and so much more. She pulled back, her hands on his chest and gazed up at him earnestly. "I want you to know something. I want you to know that if you want to go back to the FBI I'll go with you. I mean, Alex and I will. You're so good at your job, Cal, and you shouldn't have to give it up for me."

Floored and humbled in a way he'd never been before, Cal couldn't find the words to express what he was feeling. His chest felt like a steel band was wrapped around it and he had to clear his throat several times before he could speak.

"I love you so damn much. The fact that you're willing to sacrifice your own happiness for mine is just so…wow. Dammit, I'm so grateful that you're in my life and have given me another chance. But I don't want another chance with the FBI. I meant what I said—I'm staying. You're stuck with me."

Her palm cupped his cheek and he could feel the warmth of her skin against his own. "I love you too and I don't feel like I'm stuck with you. I feel like I'm very lucky."

"I'm the lucky one, and I promise to be worthy of your love. I promise to be the man that you deserve," he vowed, meaning every word from the depths of his heart and soul.

He'd come back to a heart he'd carelessly thrown away years before but he'd been given a rare second chance to find love again. Wherever Mika was, that was home.

Chapter Fifteen

M IKA STARED OUT the kitchen window that overlooked the
backyard and said one more prayer of thanks. Alex was
outside in the morning sunshine playing with Henry, his face
wreathed in smiles.

It turned out after a meal and bath the dog was actually quite
cute, although it was a mystery what breed he was. From the size
of his paws he was going to be big but she didn't mind. Alex
could play rough now and then and it was good that the canine
was of sturdy construction.

A pair of strong warm arms wrapped around her from behind and she leaned back, luxuriating in the knowledge that she
was loved and cared for, her son was safe at home, and all was
right in her world.

"I put the breakfast dishes in the dishwasher and folded the
towels in the dryer." Cal's sexy voice crooned in her ear, and
although the words were quite mundane her body responded as
if he'd paid her the most extravagant compliment. "Is there
anything else I can do to help?"

She'd had an emotional night, barely able to sleep after what
had happened, so he was spoiling her today which really wasn't

fair. He had held her all night long so he hadn't rested much either.

"You've done more than your share. I really appreciate it. I'm just going to sit here all day and watch Alex play. I suppose you think that's silly."

"I don't in the least. In fact, I might join you."

She twisted in his arms so she could look up at him. "What were you and Sheriff Dan talking about last night? You two looked deep in conversation."

Cal's smile grew and her heart skipped a beat in her chest. "He offered me a job."

"A job," she gasped, hugging him tightly. "Cal, that's wonderful. What kind of job?"

"His job. He wants to retire. He has for a long time but he hadn't found the right person to turn Applewood over to. He thinks I'm the one."

Cal would make an excellent sheriff. He was good with people and he handled a crisis like a pro – which of course he was. He was just what Applewood needed.

"That's wonderful. Are you going to take it?" Mika didn't want to push but she hoped he would. This was the perfect opportunity for him.

"There's some details to iron out but I think I will. Are you okay with that?"

"Very okay. I love the idea. But as I said before I just want you to be happy."

"I'm happier than I've ever been. I have you, Alex, Henry, and now a new job. Things are looking up."

Mika blinked back a few tears, her throat clogging with emotion. "I'm happy you're home. I never wanted to admit it but I missed you. I always hoped you'd be back someday. Here you are."

"Here I am," he agreed with a laugh and she couldn't stop smiling back at him. She was filled with life and pure unadulterated joy. "Loving you. The rest of our life starts now and that's what I want with you. A future."

For so long Mika thought love had passed her by and that she'd lost her chance to have the kind of life she'd always dreamed about. Now here it was all gift wrapped in passion and happiness and it was almost too good to be true.

But it was true. And it was all hers.

Thank you for reading Unwanted Danger

Sign up to be notified of Olivia's new releases:

http://eepurl.com/Y6aof

Acknowledgements

Thank you to Cat Johnson for granting permission for the use of the characters Jon Rudnick, Zane Alexander, Rick Mann, and Chris Cassidy and Guardian Angel Protection Services, aka GAPS, from her Hot SEALs Series world.

CAT JOHNSON'S HOT SEALS

catjohnson.net/hot-seals

Night with a SEAL – Jon

Saved by a SEAL – Zane

SEALed at Midnight – Thom

Kissed by a SEAL – Chris

Protected by a SEAL – Rick

Loved by a SEAL – Brody

Tempted by a SEAL – Mack

Wed to a SEAL – Rocky

Romanced by a SEAL – Jon & Ali

Rescued by a Hot SEAL – Grant

Betting on a Hot SEAL – Dawson

Escape with a Hot SEAL – Thom & Ginny

Matched with a Hot SEAL – Will

SEAL the Deal – Zane & Missy

About The Author

Olivia Jaymes is a wife, mother, lover of sexy romance, and caffeine addict. She lives with her husband and son in central Florida and spends her days with handsome alpha males and spunky heroines.

Olivia writes steamy romantic suspense and also contemporary romance. She is currently working on a brand new series that will debut in the fall of 2018.

Visit Olivia Jaymes at
www.OliviaJaymes.com

Other Titles by Olivia Jaymes

Danger Incorporated

Damsel In Danger

Hiding From Danger

Discarded Heart Novella

Indecent Danger

Embracing Danger

Danger In The Night

Reunited With Danger

Window to Danger

Road to Danger

Cowboy Justice Association

Cowboy Command

Justice Healed

Cowboy Truth

Cowboy Famous

Cowboy Cool

Imperfect Justice

The Deputies

Justice Inked

Justice Reborn

Vengeful Justice

Justice Divided

Military Moguls

Champagne and Bullets

Diamonds and Revolvers

Caviar and Covert Ops

Emeralds, Rubies, and Camouflage

Midnight Blue Beach

Wicked After Midnight

Midnight Of No Return

Kiss Midnight Goodbye

The Hollywood Showmance Chronicles

A Kiss For the Cameras

Swinging From A Star

Wild on the Red Carpet

Love in the Spotlight

And the Winner is

www.ingramcontent.com/pod-product-compliance
Lightning Source LLC
Chambersburg PA
CBHW020145180626
46810CB00004B/1733